A Story a Day

# 365

## Stories and Rhymes

for
every bedtime

This edition published by Parragon in 2009

Parragon
Queen Street House
4 Queen Street
Bath BA1 1HE, UK

ISBN 978-1-4075-7343-4

Printed in China

A Story a Day

# 365

Stories and Rhymes

for
every bedtime

PaRragon

Bath  New York  Singapore  Hong Kong  Cologne  Delhi  Melbourne

# CONTENTS

# JUNE

# JULY

# AUGUST

 JANUARY

# I SAW THREE SHIPS

I saw three ships come sailing by,
  Come sailing by, come sailing by;
I saw three ships come sailing by,
  On New Year's Day in the morning.

And what do you think was in them then,
  Was in them then, was in them then?
And what do you think was in them then,
  On New Year's Day in the morning?

Three pretty girls were in them then,
  Were in them then, were in them then;
Three pretty girls were in them then,
  On New Year's Day in the morning.

And one could whistle, and one could sing,
  And one could play on the violin-
Such joy there was at my wedding,
  On New Year's Day in the morning.

# I SAW A SHIP A-SAILING

I saw a ship a-sailing,
  A-sailing on the sea;
And, oh! it was all laden
  With pretty things for thee!

There were comfits in the cabin,
  And apples in the hold,
The sails were made of silk,
  And the masts were made of gold.

The four-and-twenty sailors
  That stood between the decks,
Were four-and-twenty white mice
  With chains about their necks.

The captain was a duck,
  With a packet on his back;
And when the ship began to move,
  The captain said, "Quack! quack!"

## ☸ 3 JANUARY

# THAW

Over the land freckled with show half-thawed
The speculating rooks at their nests cawed
And saw from elm-tops, delicate as flower of grass,
What we below could not see, winter pass.

Edward Thomas

12

# WEATHERS

This is the weather the cuckoo likes,
   And so do I;
When showers betumble the chestnut spikes,
   And nestlings fly;
And the little brown nightingale bills his best,
And they sit outside at "The Travellers' Rest",
And maids come forth sprig-muslin drest,
And citizens dream of the south and west,
   And so do I.

This is the weather the shepherd shuns,
   And so do I;
When beeches drip in browns and duns,
   And thresh, and ply;
And hill-hid tides throb, throe on throe,
And meadow rivulets overflow,
And drops on gate-bars hang in a row,
And rooks in families homeward go,
   And so do I.

THOMAS HARDY

13

# BLOW, BLOW, THOU WINTER WIND

Blow, blow, thou Winter wind,
Thou art not so unkind
    As man's ingratitude;
Thy tooth is not so keen,
Because thou art not seen,
    Although thy breath be rude.
Heigh ho! sing heigh ho! unto the green holly;
Most friendship is feigning, most loving mere folly:
    Then heigh ho, the holly!
    This life is most jolly.

Freeze, freeze, thou bitter sky,
Thou dost not bite so nigh
    As benefits forgot;
Though thou the waters warp,
Thy sting is not so sharp
    As friend remembered not.
Heigh ho! sing heigh ho! unto the green holly;
Most friendship is feigning, most loving mere folly:
    Then heigh ho, the holly!
    This life is most jolly.

WILLIAM SHAKESPEARE

14

## 6 JANUARY

## LITTLE WIND

Little wind, blow on the hill-top;
Little wind, blow down the plain;
Little wind, blow up the sunshine,
Little wind, blow off the rain.

KATE GREENAWAY

# GO TO BED, TOM

Go to bed, Tom,
Go to bed, Tom,
Tired or not, Tom,
Go to bed, Tom.

 JANUARY

# HIGGLEDY PIGGLEDY

Higgledy piggledy,
Here we lie,
Picked and plucked,
And put in a pie!

# WEE WILLIE WINKIE

Wee Willie Winkie runs through the town,
Up-stairs and down-stairs in his nightgown,
Peeping through the keyhole, crying through the lock,
"Are the children in their beds, it's past eight o'clock?"

# THREE WISE MEN OF GOTHAM

Three wise men of Gotham
Went to sea in a bowl:
And if the bowl had been stronger,
My song would have been longer.

**11 JANUARY**

# JACKANORY

I'll tell you a story
Of Jackanory,
And now my story's begun;
I'll tell you another
Of Jack his brother,
And now my story's done.

# FOR EVERY EVIL UNDER THE SUN

For every evil under the sun,
There is a remedy, or there is none.
If there be one, try and find it;
If there be none, never mind it.

13 JANUARY

# SALLY GO ROUND THE MOON

Sally go round the moon,
Sally go round the stars;
Sally go round the moon
On a Sunday afternoon.

## ⟨14⟩ JANUARY

# STAR LIGHT, STAR BRIGHT

Star light, star bright,
First star I see tonight,
I wish I may, I wish I might,
Have the wish I wish tonight.

# THE SAINT AND GOD 'S CREATURES

Long ago, at the time when the first Christians were building their churches in Wales, there lived a young lad called Baglan. He worked for an old holy man, who was struck by the boy's kindness, and his eagerness to serve God.

One day it was cold and the holy man wanted a fire in his room. So he asked Baglan to move some hot coals to make a fire and to his surprise, the boy carried in some red-hot coals in the fabric of his cloak. When the boy had set the coals in the fire, not a bit of his cloak was burned or even singed.

The old holy man knew a miracle when he saw one. "You are meant to do great works for God," said the holy man. "The time is passed when you should stay here serving me." And the old man produced a crook with a shining brass handle and offered it to the lad. "Take this crook, and set off on a journey. The crook will lead your steps to a place where you must build a church. Look out for a tree which bears three different kinds of fruit. Then you will know that you have come to the right spot."

So the young man took the crook and walked southwards a long way. In time Baglan came to a tree. Around the roots of the tree a family of pigs were grubbing for food. In the tree's trunk had nested a colony of bees. And in the branches of the tree was a nest where a pair of crows were feeding their young.

Baglan sensed that this must be the right place. But the tree grew on sloping land, which did not seem good for building. So the young man looked around until he found a nearby area which was flat, and there he began to build his church.

He worked hard on the first day, digging the foundations, and building the first walls, and he slept well after his labours. But in the morning he was dismayed to see that the walls had all fallen down and water was seeping into the foundation

trenches. So the next day, he worked still harder, and raised the walls stronger and higher than before. But when Baglan awoke the next morning, again the walls had been flattened. He tried once more, putting still greater effort into making his building strong. But again the walls were laid low, and Baglan began to despair of ever finishing his church.

Baglan kneeled down to pray, and then he sat down to think. Perhaps he was not building in exactly the right place. So he moved his site nearer the tree, for the holy man had told him to build where he found the tree with three fruits. Straight

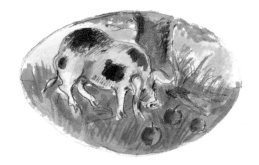

away things began to go better. The pigs, rooting with their snouts, helped him dig out the new foundations. The bees gave him honey. Even the crows offered him crusts of bread that they had scavenged. And this time, Baglan's work was lasting.

So he built and built until his walls surrounded the old tree, leaving windows for the pigs and bees, and a hole in the roof for the birds to fly in and out. As a result, his church looked

rather unusual, but he knew that it was right.

The young man kneeled down and prayed to God in thanks. And when he finished his prayer, he saw that all the animals – the pigs, and the bees, and the crows – had also fallen still and silent, as if they, too, were thanking God that the work was completed.

After that, Baglan was always kind to the animals, and taught others to show kindness to them also. His crook may have been a holy relic that guided him to the tree, but even it could be used to scratch the back of the great boar.

# WHEN FAMED KING ARTHUR RULED THIS LAND

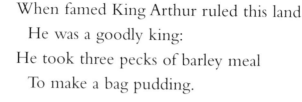

When famed King Arthur ruled this land
  He was a goodly king:
He took three pecks of barley meal
  To make a bag pudding.

A rare pudding the king did make,
  And stuffed it well with plums;
And in it put such lumps of fat,
  As big as my two thumbs.

The king and queen did eat thereof,
  And noblemen beside,
And what they could not eat that night
  The queen next morning fried.

 JANUARY

# WHAT IS THE RHYME FOR PORRINGER?

What is the rhyme for *porringer*?
The King he had a daughter fair,
And gave the Prince of Orange her.

 JANUARY

# GREY GOOSE AND GANDER

Grey goose and gander,
  Waft your wings together,
And carry the good king's daughter
  Over the one strand river.

**19 JANUARY**

# OLIVER TWIST

Oliver Twist
You can't do this,
So what's the use
Of trying?
Touch your toe,
Touch your knee,
Clap your hands,
Away we go.

# A SAILOR WENT TO SEA

A sailor went to sea, sea, sea,

To see what he could see, see, see,

But all that he could see, see, see,

Was the bottom of the deep blue sea, sea, sea.

# LITTLE SALLY WATERS

Little Sally Waters,
Sitting in the sun,
Crying and weeping,
For a young man.
Rise, Sally, rise,
Dry your weeping eyes,
Fly to the east,
Fly to the west,
Fly to the one you love the best.

# MR. NOBODY

Mr. Nobody is a nice young man,

He comes to the door with his hat in his hand.

Down she comes, all dressed in silk,

A rose in her bosom, as white as milk.

She takes off her gloves, she shows me her ring,

Tomorrow, tomorrow, the wedding begins.

# HAVE YOU SEEN THE MUFFIN MAN

Have you seen the muffin man, the muffin man, the
muffin man,
Have you seen the muffin man that lives in Drury
Lane O?
Yes, I've seen the muffin man, the muffin man, the
muffin man;
Yes, I've seen the muffin man who lives in Drury
Lane O.

# OLD ROGER IS DEAD

Old Roger is dead and
   gone to his grave,
H'm ha! gone to his grave.

They planted an apple tree
   over his head,
H'm ha! over his head.

The apples were ripe
   and ready to fall,
H'm ha! ready to fall.

There came an old woman
   and picked them all up,
H'm ha! picked them all up.

Old Roger jumped up and
   gave her a knock,
H'm ha! gave her a knock.

Which made the old woman
   go hippity hop,
H'm ha! hippity hop!

33

 JANUARY

# SNEEZE ON MONDAY

Sneeze on Monday, sneeze for danger;
Sneeze on Tuesday, kiss a stranger;
Sneeze on Wednesday, get a letter;
Sneeze on Thursday, something better;
Sneeze on Friday, sneeze for sorrow;
Sneeze on Saturday, see your sweetheart
  tomorrow.

 JANUARY

# SEE A PIN AND PICK IT UP

See a pin and pick it up,
All the day you'll have good luck;
See a pin and let it lay,
Bad luck you'll have all the day!

34

# 27 JANUARY

# RAIN, RAIN, GO AWAY

Rain, rain, go away,
Come again another day.

 JANUARY

Hop-o'-my-thumb and little Jack Horner,
  What do you mean by tearing and fighting?
Sturdy dog Trot close round the corner,
  I never caught him growling and biting.

 JANUARY

I know a baby, such a baby,—
  Round blue eyes and cheeks of pink,
Such an elbow furrowed with dimples,
  Such a wrist where creases sink.

 JANUARY

  Lullaby, oh lullaby!
Flowers are closed and lambs are sleeping;
  Lullaby, oh lullaby!
Stars are up, the moon is peeping;
  Lullaby, oh lullaby!
While the birds are silence keeping,
  (Lullaby, oh lullaby!)
Sleep, my baby, fall a-sleeping,
  Lullaby, oh lullaby!

#  JANUARY

What does the bee do?
  Bring home honey.
And what does Father do?
  Bring home money.
And what does Mother do?
  Lay out the money.
And what does baby do?
  Eat up the honey.

##  FEBRUARY

The dog lies in his kennel,
  And Puss purrs on the rug,
And baby perches on my knee
  For me to love and hug.

##  FEBRUARY

Pat the dog and stroke the cat,
  Each in its degree;
And cuddle and kiss my baby,
  And baby kiss me.

# THE LION AND THE UNICORN

The lion and the unicorn
  Were fighting for the crown:
The lion beat the unicorn
  All round the town.
Some gave them white bread,
  Some gave them brown:
Some gave them plum-cake
  And drummed them out of town.

# POP GOES THE WEASEL

Up and down the City Road
  In and out the Eagle,
That's the way the money goes,
  Pop goes the weasel!

Half a pound of tuppenny rice,
  Half a pound of treacle,
Mix it up and make it nice,
  Pop goes the weasel!

Every night when I go out
  The monkey's on the table;
Take a stick and knock it off,
  Pop goes the weasel!

# THERE WAS AN OLD MAN WITH A BEARD

There was an old Man with a beard,
Who said, "It is just as I feared!—
Two Owls and a Hen, four Larks and a Wren
Have all built their nests in my beard!"

EDWARD LEAR

FEBRUARY

# THERE WAS AN OLD MAN FROM PERU

There was an old man from Peru
Who dreamed he was eating his shoe.
He woke in a fright
In the middle of the night
And found it was perfectly true.

ANONYMOUS
ENGLISH

40

# OZYMANDIAS

I met a traveller from an antique land
Who said: Two vast and trunkless legs of stone
Stand in the desert....Near them, on the sand,
Half sunk, a shattered visage lies, whose frown,
And wrinkled lip, and sneer of cold command,
Tell that its sculptor well those passions read
Which yet survive, stamped on these lifeless things,
The hand that mocked them, and the heart that fed:
And on the pedestal these words appear:
"My name is Ozymandias, king of kings:
Look on my works, ye Mighty, and despair!"
Nothing beside remains. Round the decay
Of that colossal wreck, boundless and bare
The lone and level sands stretch far away.

PERCY BYSSHE SHELLEY

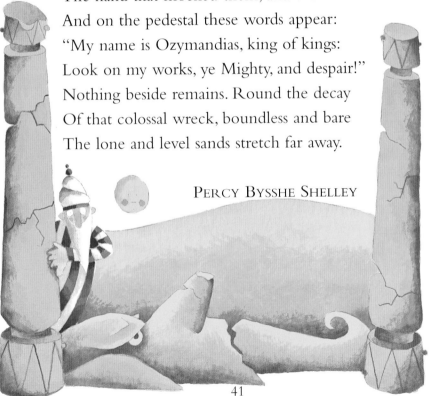

 FEBRUARY

# WHEN THAT I WAS AND A LITTLE TINY BOY

When that I was and a little tiny boy,
  With hey, ho, the wind and the rain;
A foolish thing was but a toy,
  For the rain it raineth every day.

But when I came to man's estate,
  With hey, ho, the wind and the rain;
'Gainst knaves and thieves men shut their gate,
  For the rain it raineth every day.

A great while ago the world begun,
  With hey, ho, the wind and the rain;
But that's all one, our play is done,
  And we'll strive to please you every day.

WILLIAM SHAKESPEARE

 FEBRUARY

# I EAT MY PEAS WITH HONEY

I eat my peas with honey,
I've done it all my life,
It makes the peas taste funny,
But it keeps them on my knife.

ANONYMOUS
AMERICAN

FEBRUARY

# BREAD AND MILK FOR BREAKFAST

Bread and milk for breakfast,
And woollen frocks to wear,
And a crumb for robin redbreast
On the cold days of the year.

CHRISTINA ROSSETTI

# WINDY NIGHTS

Whenever the moon and stars are set,
  Whenever the wind is high,
All night long in the dark and wet,
  A man goes riding by
Late in the night when the fires are out,
Why does he gallop and gallop about?

Whenever the trees are crying aloud,
  And ships are tossed at sea,
By, on the highway, low and loud,
  By at the gallop goes he.
By at the gallop he goes, and then
By he comes back at the gallop again.

ROBERT LOUIS STEVENSON

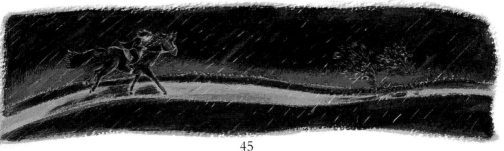

# MUNACHAR AND MANACHAR

There were once two little fellows called Munachar and Manachar. They liked to pick raspberries, but Manachar always ate them all. Munachar got so fed up with this that he said he would look for a rod to make a gibbet to hang Manachar.

Soon, Munachar came to a rod. "What do you want?" said the rod. "A rod, to make a gibbet," replied Munachar.

"You won't get me," said the rod, "unless you can get an axe to cut me." So Munachar went to find an axe. "What do you want?" said the axe. "I am looking for an axe, to cut a rod, to make a gibbet," replied Munachar.

"You won't get me," said the axe, "unless you can get a stone to sharpen me." So Munachar went to find a stone. "What do you want?" said the stone. "I am looking for a stone, to sharpen an axe, to cut a rod, to make a gibbet," replied Munachar.

"You won't get me," said the stone, "unless you can get water to wet me." So Munachar went to find water. "What do you want?" said the water. "I am looking for water to wet a stone, to sharpen an axe, to cut a rod, to make a gibbet," replied Munachar.

"You won't get me," said the water, "unless you can get a deer who will swim me." So Munachar went to look for a deer. "What do you want?" said the deer. "I am looking for a deer, to swim some water, to wet a stone, to sharpen an axe, to cut a rod, to make a gibbet," replied Munachar.

"You won't get me," said the deer, "unless you can get a hound who will hunt me." So Munachar went to look for a hound. "What do you want?" said the hound. "I am looking for a hound, to hunt a deer, to swim some water, to wet a stone, to sharpen an axe, to cut a rod, to make a gibbet," replied Munachar.

"You won't get me," said the hound, "unless you can get some butter to put in my claw." So Munachar went to look for some butter. "What do you want?" said the butter. "I am looking for some butter to put in the claw of a hound, to hunt a deer, to swim some water, to wet a stone, to sharpen an axe, to cut a rod, to make a gibbet," replied Munachar.

"You won't get me," said the butter, "unless you can get a cat who can scrape me." So Munachar went to look for a cat.

"What do you want?" said the cat. "I am looking for a cat to scrape some butter, to put in the claw of a hound, to hunt a deer, to swim some water, to wet a stone, to sharpen an axe, to cut a rod, to make a gibbet, " replied Munachar.

"You won't get me," said the cat, "unless you can get some milk to feed me." So Munachar went to get some milk. "What do you want?" said the milk. "I am looking for some milk, to feed a cat, to scrape some butter, to put in the claw of a hound, to hunt a deer, to swim some water, to wet a stone, to sharpen an axe, to cut a rod, to make a gibbet," replied Munachar.

"You won't get me," said the milk, "unless you can bring me some straw from those threshers over there." So Munachar went to ask the threshers. "What do you want?" said the threshers. "I am looking for some straw, to give to the milk, to feed a cat, to scrape some butter, to put in the claw of a hound, to hunt a deer, to swim some water, to wet a stone, to sharpen an axe, to cut a rod, to make a gibbet," replied Munachar.

"You won't get any straw," said the threshers, "unless you

bring some flour to bake a cake from the miller next door." So
Munachar went to ask the miller. "What do you want?" said
the miller. "I am looking for some flour to bake a cake, to give
to the threshers, to get some straw, to give to the milk, to feed
a cat, to scrape some butter, to put in the claw of a hound, to
hunt a deer, to swim some water, to wet a stone, to sharpen an
axe, to cut a rod, to make a gibbet," replied Munachar.

"You'll get no flour ," said the miller, "unless you fill this sieve
with water." Some crows flew over crying "Daub! Daub!" So
Munachar daubed some clay on the sieve, so it would hold
water.

And he took the water to the miller, who gave him the flour;
he gave the flour to the threshers, who gave him some straw;
he took the straw to the cow, who gave him some milk; he
took the milk to the cat, who scraped some butter; he gave the
butter to the hound, who hunted the deer; the deer swam the
water; the water wet the stone; the stone sharpened the axe;
the axe cut the rod; the rod made a gibbet – and when
Munachar was ready to hang Manachar, he found that
Manachar had BURST!

 FEBRUARY

# I LOVE LITTLE KITTY

I love little kitty, her coat is so warm;
And if I don't hurt her she'll do me no harm.
So I'll not pull her tail nor drive her away,
But kitty and I very gently will play.

 FEBRUARY

# PUSSY-CAT MOLE

Pussy-cat Mole,
Jumped over a coal,
And in her best petticoat burnt a great hole.
Poor pussy's weeping, she'll have no more milk,
Until her best petticoat's mended with silk.

# 15 FEBRUARY

# PUSSY-CAT, PUSSY-CAT

Pussy-cat, pussy-cat, where have you been?
I've been to London to see the Queen.
Pussy-cat, pussy-cat, what did you there?
I frightened a little mouse under her chair.

# JACK, JACK, THE BREAD'S A-BURNING

Jack, Jack, the bread's a-burning,
All to a cinder;
If you don't come and fetch it out
We'll throw it through the window.

**17 FEBRUARY**

# JACK AND GUY

Jack and Guy
  Went out in the rye,
And they found a little boy with one black eye.
Come, says Jack, let's knock him on the head.
No, says Guy, let's buy him some bread;
You buy one loaf and I'll buy two,
And we'll bring him up as other folk do.

# JACK AND JILL

Jack and Jill went up the hill
  To fetch a pail of water;
Jack fell down and broke his crown,
  And Jill came tumbling after.

Up Jack got, and home did trot,
  As fast as he could caper,
Went to bed to mend his head
  With vinegar and brown paper.

# LITTLE JACK JINGLE

Little Jack Jingle,
He used to live single:
But when he got tired of this kind of life,
He left off being single, and lived with his wife.

# HARRY PARRY

O rare Harry Parry,
When will you marry?
When apples and pears are ripe.
I'll come to your wedding,
Without any bidding,
And dance and sing all the night.

# YOUNG ROGER CAME TAPPING

Young Roger came tapping at Dolly's window,
  Thumpaty, thumpaty, thump!
He asked for admittance, she answered him "No!"
  Frumpaty, frumpaty, frump!

"No, no, Roger, no! as you came you may go!"
  Stumpaty, stumpaty, stump!

# 22 FEBRUARY

# SOLOMON GRUNDY

Solomon Grundy,
Born on Monday,
Christened on Tuesday,
Married on
Wednesday,
Sick on Thursday,
Worse on Friday,
Died on Saturday,
Buried on Sunday,
That was the end
Of Solomon Grundy.

# OLD KING COLE

Old King Cole
Was a merry old soul,
And a merry old soul was he;
He called for his pipe,
And he called for his bowl,
And he called for his fiddlers three.
Every fiddler had a fine fiddle,
And a very fine fiddle had he;
Twee tweedle dee, tweedle dee, went the fiddlers,
   Very merry men are we;
   Oh there's none so rare
   As can compare
With King Cole and his fiddlers three.

# BOBBIE SHAFTOE'S GONE TO SEA

Bobbie Shaftoe's gone to sea,
Silver buckles at his knee;
When he comes back he'll marry me,
Bonny Bobbie Shaftoe!

 FEBRUARY

# PUSSY HAS A WHISKERED FACE

Pussy has a whiskered face,
Kitty has such pretty ways;
Doggie scampers when I call,
And has a heart to love us all.

 FEBRUARY

# JOHNNY SHALL HAVE A NEW BONNET

Johnny shall have a new bonnet,
And Johnny shall go to the fair,
And Johnny shall have a blue ribbon
To tie up his bonny brown hair.

# THE MISSING KETTLE

There was a woman who lived on the island of Sanntraigh, and she had only a kettle to hang over the fire to boil her water and cook her food. Every day one of the fairy folk would come to take the kettle. She would slip into the house quietly without saying a word, and grab hold of the kettle handle.

Each time this happened, the kettle handle made a clanking noise and the woman looked up and recited this rhyme:

> A smith is able to make
> Cold iron hot with coal.
> The due of a kettle is bones,
> And to bring it back again whole.

Then the fairy would fly away with the kettle and the woman would not see it again until later in the day, when the fairy brought it back, filled with flesh and bones.

There came at last a day when the woman had to leave home and go on the ferry across to the mainland. She turned to her husband, who was making a rope of heather to keep the thatch on the roof. "Will you say the rhyme that I say when the fairy comes for the kettle?" Her husband said that he would recite the rhyme just as she did, and went back to his work.

After the woman had left to
catch the boat, the fairy
arrived as usual, and the
husband saw her come to the
door. When he saw her he
started to feel afraid, for
unlike his wife he had had
no contact with the little
people. "If I lock the cottage
door," he reasoned to himself,
"she will go away and leave
the kettle, and it will be just
as if she had never come." So
the husband locked the door
and did not open it when the
fairy tried to come in.

But instead of going away,
the fairy flew up to the hole
in the roof where the smoke
from the fire escaped, and
before the husband knew
what was happening, the
creature had made the kettle
jump right up and out of the

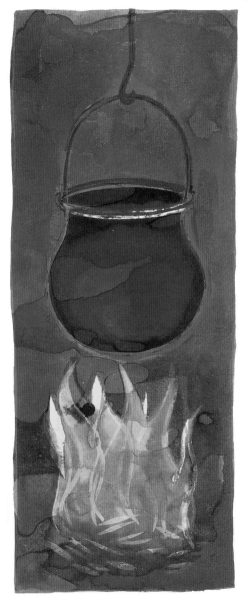

61

hole. The fairy made away with the kettle before he knew what to do.

When his wife returned that evening, there was no kettle to be seen.

"What have you done with my kettle?" asked the woman.

"I've done nothing with it," said the husband. "But I took fright when the fairy came, closed the door to her, she took the kettle through the roof, and now it is gone."

"You pathetic wretch! Can't you even mind the kettle when I go out for the day?"

The husband tried to tell his wife that the fairy might return the kettle the next day, but the woman would hear nothing of it. Off she went straight away to the knoll where the fairies lived, to see if she could get back the kettle herself.

It was quite dark when she reached the fairies' knoll. The hillside opened to her and when she went in she saw only an old fairy sitting in the corner. The woman supposed that the others were out at their nightly mischief. Soon she found her kettle, and noticed that it still contained the remains of the food the little people had cooked in it.

She picked up the kettle and ran back down the lane, when she heard the sound of dogs chasing her. The old fairy must have let them loose. Thinking quickly, she took out some of the food from the kettle, threw it to the dogs, and hurried on.

This slowed down the dogs, and when they began to catch her up again, she threw down more food. Finally, when she got near her own gate, she poured out the rest of the food, hoping that the dogs would not come into her own house. Then she ran inside and closed the door.

Every day after that the woman watched for the fairy coming to take her kettle. But the little creature never came again.

# OLD JOE BROWN

Old Joe Brown, he had a wife,
　She was all of eight feet tall.
She slept with her head in the kitchen,
　And her feet stuck out in the hall.

 MARCH

# DANDY

I had a dog and his name was Dandy,
His tail was long and his legs were bandy,
His eyes were brown and his coat was sandy,
The best in the world was my dog Dandy!

 MARCH

# FUZZY WUZZY

Fuzzy Wuzzy was a bear,
    A bear was Fuzzy Wuzzy.
When Fuzzy Wuzzy lost his hair
    He wasn't fuzzy, was he?

# THE SWING

How do you like to go up in a swing,
　Up in the air so blue?
Oh, I do think it the pleasantest thing
　Ever a child can do!

Up in the air and over the wall,
　Till I can see so wide,
Rivers and trees and cattle and all
　Over the countryside–

Till I look down on the garden green,
　Down on the roof so brown–
Up in the air I go flying again,
　Up in the air and down!

ROBERT LOUIS STEVENSON

# THE CITY CHILD

Dainty little maiden, whither would you wander?
  Whither from this pretty home, the home where
    mother dwells?
"Far and far away," said the dainty little maiden,
"All among the gardens, auriculas, anemones,
  Roses and lilies and Canterbury-bells."

Dainty little maiden, whither would you wander?
  Whither from this pretty house, this city house
    of ours?
"Far and far away," said the dainty little maiden,
"All among the meadows, the clover and the clematis,
  Daisies and kingcups and honeysuckle-flowers."

ALFRED, LORD TENNYSON

 **5 MARCH**

# TOMMY SNOOKS AND BESSY BROOKS

As Tommy Snooks and Bessy Brooks
Were walking out one Sunday,
Says Tommy Snooks to Bessy Brooks,
"Tomorrow will be Monday."

 **6 MARCH**

# LITTLE JUMPING JOAN

Here am I, little jumping Joan.
When nobody's with me,
I'm always alone.

# THERE WAS A LITTLE GIRL

There was a little girl, and she had a little curl
  Right in the middle of her forehead;
When she was good she was very, very good,
  But when she was bad she was horrid.

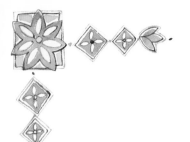

 **8 MARCH**

# ANNA BANANA

Anna Banana
Played the piano;
The piano broke
And Anna choked.

**9 MARCH**

# LUCY LOCKET

Lucy Locket lost her pocket,
  Kitty Fisher found it,
But not a penny was there in it,
  Just the binding round it.

# LITTLE MISS MUFFET

Little Miss Muffet
Sat on a tuffet,
Eating her curds and whey;
There came a great spider,
Who sat down beside her,
And frightened Miss Muffet away.

# THE BLACK LAD MacCRIMMON

There was once a young man called the Black Lad MacCrimmon. He was the youngest of three brothers and he was the most down-trodden of the three. His elder brothers were always favoured by their father, and were always given more food, and allowed more enjoyment, than the Black Lad. The Black Lad, on the other hand, was always given the hardest jobs to do when the four were working together.

The father and the elder brothers were all great pipers, and they had a fine set of pipes that they liked to play. The Black Lad would have liked to have played the pipes too, but he was never allowed. Always the brothers took up too much time with their playing to give the young lad a chance.

In those days, people said that the greatest musicians of all were the fairy folk. The Black Lad hoped that one day he would meet one of the little people and they would teach him to master the pipes.

The day came that the lad's father and his two brothers were getting ready to go to the fair. The Black Lad wanted to go

too, but they would not take him. So the lad stayed at home, and when they were gone, he decided to take up the chanter from the set of pipes and see if he could play a tune.

After a while of practising, the lad began to pick out a tune on the chanter. He was starting to enjoy himself, and was so absorbed in what he was doing that he did not notice that someone was watching him and listening.

Suddenly a voice spoke in his ear: "You are doing well with your music, lad." It was none other than the Banshee from the castle.

"Which would you prefer," continued the Banshee. "Skill without success or success without skill?"

73

The lad replied that what he wanted most of all was skill, it did not matter about success. The Banshee smiled, as if she approved of the answer, and pulled a long hair from her head. This she wound around the reed of the chanter. Then she turned to the Black Lad MacCrimmon. "Now put your fingers on the holes of the chanter, and I will place my fingers over yours. I will guide you. When I lift one of my fingers, you lift yours that is beneath it. Think of a tune that you would like to play, and I will help you play. And my skill will rub off on you."

So the lad began to play, guided by the Banshee as she had told him. Soon he was playing with great skill, and he could master any tune that he thought of.

"Indeed you are the King of the Pipers," said the Banshee. "There has been none better before you, and none better shall come after." And with this blessing, the Banshee went on her way back to the castle.

The Black Lad carried on playing when she had left, and he could play all the tunes that he tried. When his father and

brothers returned, they could
hear him playing as they came
along the road, but by the time
they entered the house, the lad
had put away the pipes, and was
acting as if nothing at all had
happened.

None of them mentioned that
they had heard music when they
came in, but the lad's father took
down the pipes, and played as
usual. Then he handed them to
his first son, who played and passed them to the second son.
But instead of putting the pipes away after his second son had
played, old MacCrimmon handed the pipes to his youngest
son. "Now take the pipes, for no longer shall you spend all day
doing the hardest of the work and eating the meanest of the
food."

When the lad played, they heard that he was far better than
any of them. "There is no longer any point in our playing,"
said the father to the two eldest sons. "The lad is truly King of
the Pipers." And the lad's brothers knew that what their father
said was true.

 MARCH

# TOM, TOM, THE PIPER'S SON

Tom, Tom, the piper's son,
Stole a pig, and away did run.
The pig was eat, and Tom was beat,
And Tom went roaring down the street.

 MARCH

# TOM, HE WAS A PIPER'S SON

Tom, he was a piper's son,
He learnt to play when he was young,
And all the tune that he could play,
Was, "Over the hills and far away."

*Over the hills and a great way off,*
*The wind shall blow my topknot off.*

Tom with his pipe made such a noise
That he pleased both the girls and boys,
And they all stopped to hear him play
"Over the hills and far away."

*Over the hills and a great way off,*
*The wind shall blow my topknot off.*

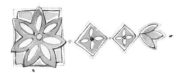

 MARCH

# ELSIE MARLEY

Elsie Marley is grown so fine,
She won't get up to serve the swine,
But lies in bed till eight or nine,
And surely she does take her time.

## 15 MARCH

# MARY, MARY

Mary, Mary, quite contrary,
How does your garden grow?
With silver bells, and cockle shells,
And pretty maids all in a row.

### 🗓16 MARCH

# POLLY, PUT THE KETTLE ON

Polly, put the kettle on,
Polly, put the kettle on,
Polly, put the kettle on,
    And we'll all have tea.

Sukey, take it off again,
Sukey, take it off again,
Sukey, take it off again,
    They're all gone away.

# A PRETTY LITTLE GIRL

A pretty little girl in a round-eared cap
I met in the streets the other day;
  She gave me such a thump,
  That my heart it went bump;
I thought I should have fainted away!
I thought I should have fainted away!

# THE FARMER AND THE GOAT GIRL

There was once a farmer called Cadwalader. Unlike all his neighbours, who were sheep farmers, Cadwalader had a large flock of goats. Of all his goats he had a special favourite that he called Jenny, and Jenny was the whitest and most beautiful of all his flock.

For many years Jenny was Cadwalader's best milk-producer, and she was always obedient, unlike some of the stubborn

creatures in his flock. Then, one day, Jenny bolted from the field and ran away. Up the nearest mountain she went, and seemed not to be stopping, so Cadwalader gave chase.

They climbed higher and higher, Jenny always slightly ahead. When it seemed as if the farmer would catch her, she jumped on to a nearby crag, leaving Cadwalader stranded.

Not only did the farmer feel stupid, stuck on the mountain like this, he also collected bruises and sprains as he clambered among the rocks. Finally, he had had enough, and he picked up a stone and hurled it at the goat in frustration as she was jumping another chasm.

The stone hit Jenny in the side, and, bleating loudly, she fell far down into the gap between the rocks. Straight away Cadwalader was full of remorse. It was only in a moment of frustration that he had wanted to hurt the animal, and now his only wish was to see that she was still alive. He clambered down to the rocky gap where she lay, and saw that, although she was still breathing, she was badly injured. He did his best to make her comfortable, and tears of sadness formed in his eyes as he saw how she was hurt.

It was now dark, but the moon appeared between the rocks and shed its light on the scene. As the moon rose, the goat turned into a beautiful young woman who was lying there before Cadwalader. He looked in bafflement at her brown eyes and soft hair, and

found that not only was she beautiful, she was also well and looked pleased to see him. "So, my dear Cadwalader," she said. "At long last I can speak to you."

Cadwalader did not know what to make of all this. When the young woman spoke, there seemed to be a bleat in her voice; when she held his hand, it felt like a hoof. Was she goat or girl, or some strange mixture of the two?

As she led him towards an outcrop of rock, Cadwalader felt he was heading into danger. As they rounded a corner, they found themselves surrounded by a flock of goats — not the tame creatures Cadwalader was used to, but large wild goats,

many of which had long horns and beards. Jenny led him to the largest goat of all, and bowed, as if he were a king.

"Is this the man you want?" the goat asked Jenny.

"Yes, he is the one."

"Not a very fine specimen," said the goat-king. "I had hoped for something better."

"He will be better afterwards," replied Jenny.

Cadwalader wondered what was going to happen, and looked around him in fear. Then the goat-king turned to Cadwalader.

"Will you, Cadwalader, take this she-goat to be your wife?"

"No, my lord. I want nothing to do with goats ever again." And with that, Cadwalader turned and ran for his life. He was fast, but not fast enough for the great goat-king. Coming up behind Cadwalader, the huge billy goat gave the farmer such a tremendous butt that Cadwalader fell headlong down the crag, rolling and falling, falling and rolling, until he came to a stop, unconscious, right at the bottom of the mountain.

There Cadwalader lay for the rest of the night, until he woke, aching from head to toe, at dawn. He limped home to his farm, where his goats bleated in welcome. But Cadwalader wanted to be a goat farmer no more. He drove his goats to market, and bought a flock of sheep, just like his neighbours.

 MARCH

# HURT NO LIVING THING

Hurt no living thing,
 Ladybird nor butterfly,
Nor moth with dusty wing,
Nor cricket chirping cheerily,
Nor grasshopper, so light of leap,
 Nor dancing gnat,
 Nor beetle fat,
Nor harmless worms that creep.

CHRISTINA ROSSETTI

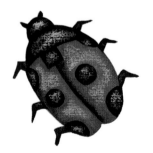

 MARCH

# THE COW

The friendly cow all red and white,
  I love with all my heart:
She gives me cream with all her might,
  To eat with apple tart.

She wanders lowing here and there,
  And yet she cannot stray,
All in the pleasant open air,
  The pleasant light of day;

And blown by all the winds that pass
  And wet with all the showers,
She walks among the meadow grass
  And eats the meadow flowers.

ROBERT LOUIS STEVENSON

# TO A BUTTERFLY

I've watched you now a full half-hour,
Self-poised upon that yellow flower;
And, little Butterfly! indeed
I know not if you sleep or feed.
How motionless!—not frozen seas
More motionless! And then
What joy awaits you, when the breeze
Hath found you out among the trees,
And calls you forth again!

This plot of orchard-ground is ours;
My trees they are, my Sister's flowers.
Here rest your wings when they are weary;
Here lodge as in a sanctuary!
Come often to us, fear no wrong;
Sit near us on the bough!
We'll talk of sunshine and of song,
And summer days, when we were young;
Sweet childish days, that were as long
As twenty days are now.

WILLIAM WORDSWORTH

88

# CATERPILLAR

Brown and furry
Caterpillar in a hurry,
Take your walk
To the shady leaf, or stalk,
Or what not,
Which may be the chosen spot.
No toad spy you,
Hovering bird of prey pass by you;
Spin and die,
To live again a butterfly.

CHRISTINA ROSSETTI

# WASH, HANDS, WASH

Wash, hands, wash,
  Daddy's gone to plough;
If you want your hands washed,
  Have them washed now.

 MARCH

# CLAP HANDS

Clap hands for Daddy coming
Down the wagon way,
With a pocketful of money
And a cartload of hay.

# THE GREAT BROWN OWL

The brown owl sits in the ivy bush,
   And she looketh wondrous wise,
With a horny beak beneath her cowl,
   And a pair of large round eyes.

She sat all day on the selfsame spray,
   From sunrise till sunset;
And the dim, grey light it was all too bright
   For the owl to see in yet.

"Jenny Owlet, Jenny Owlet," said a merry little bird,
   "They say you're wondrous wise;
But I don't think you see, though you're looking at *me*
   With your large, round, shining eyes."

But night came soon, and the pale white moon
   Rolled high up in the skies;
And the great brown owl flew away in her cowl,
   With her large, round, shining eyes.

AUNT EFFIE (JANE EUPHEMIA BROWNE)

# THE OWL

When cats run home and light is come,
  And dew is cold upon the ground,
And the far-off stream is dumb,
  And the whirring sail goes round,
  And the whirring sail goes round;
  Alone and warming his five wits,
  The white owl in the belfry sits.

When merry milkmaids click the latch,
  And rarely smells the new-mown hay,
And the cock hath sung beneath the thatch
  Twice or thrice his roundelay,
  Twice or thrice his roundelay;
  Alone and warming his five wits,
  The white owl in the belfry sits.

ALFRED, LORD TENNYSON

93

# LITTLE TROTTY WAGTAIL

Little Trotty Wagtail, he went in the rain,
And twittering, tottering sideways, he ne'er got
  straight again;
He stooped to get a worm, and looked up to get a fly,
And then he flew away ere his feathers they were dry.

Little Trotty Wagtail, he waddled in the mud,
And left his little foot-marks, trample where he would,
He waddled in the water-pudge, and waggle went his tail,
And chirrupped up his wings to dry upon the garden rail.

Little Trotty Wagtail, you nimble all about,
And in the dimpling water-pudge you waddle in and out;
Your home is nigh at hand and in the warm pig-stye;
So, little Master Wagtail, I'll bid you a good-bye.

JOHN CLARE

# EPIGRAM

*Engraved on the Collar of a Dog which I Gave to His*
*Royal Highness*

I am his Highness' Dog at Kew:
Pray tell me, sir, whose dog are you?

ALEXANDER POPE

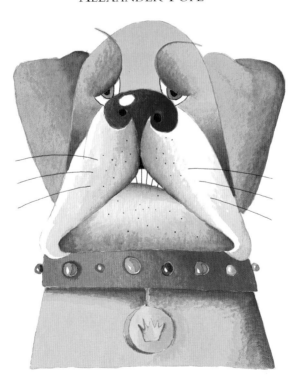

# BLOW, WIND, BLOW!

Blow, wind, blow! and go, mill, go!
That the miller may grind his corn;
  That the baker may take it,
  And into rolls make it,
And send us some hot in the morn.

## MARCH

# PAT-A-CAKE, PAT-A-CAKE, BAKER'S MAN!

Pat-a-cake, pat-a-cake, baker's man!
  Bake me a cake, as fast as you can;
Pat it and prick it, and mark it with T,
  And put it aside for Tommy and me.

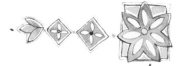

# HOT-CROSS BUNS

Hot–Cross Buns!
Hot–Cross Buns!
One a penny, two a penny,
Hot–Cross Buns!

Hot–Cross Buns!
Hot–Cross Buns!
If you have no daughters
Give them to your sons.

 APRIL

# ONCE I SAW A LITTLE BIRD

Once I saw a little bird
Come hop, hop, hop;
So I cried, "Little bird,
Will you stop, stop, stop?"
And was going to the window,
To say, "How do you do?"
But he shook his little tail,
And far away he flew.

98

 APRIL

# JAY-BIRD

Jay-bird, jay-bird, settin' on a rail,
Pickin' his teeth with the end of his tail;
Mulberry leaves and calico sleeves–
All school teachers are hard to please.

 APRIL

# BIRDS OF A FEATHER

Birds of a feather flock together
And so will pigs and swine;
Rats and mice shall have their choice,
And so shall I have mine.

# TIGGY-TOUCHWOOD

Tiggy-tiggy-touchwood, my black hen,
She lays eggs for gentlemen,
Sometimes nine and sometimes ten,
Tiggy-tiggy-touchwood, my black hen.

# I HAD A LITTLE HEN

5 APRIL

I had a little hen, the prettiest ever seen,
She washed me the dishes, and kept the house clean:
She went to the mill to fetch me some flour,
She brought it home in less than an hour;
She baked me my bread, she brewed me my ale,
She sat by the fire and told many a fine tale.

# MRS HEN

Chook, chook, chook, chook, chook,
  Good morning, Mrs Hen.
How many chickens have you got?
  Madam, I've got ten.

Four of them are yellow,
  And four of them are brown,
And two of them are speckled red,
  The nicest in the town.

 APRIL

Seldom 'can't', seldom 'don't';
Never 'shan't', never 'won't'.

 APRIL

Oh fair to see
Bloom-laden cherry tree,
  Arrayed in sunny white,
  An April day's delight;
Oh fair to see!

Oh fair to see
Fruit-laden cherry tree,
  With balls of shining red
  Decking a leafy head;
Oh fair to see!

 APRIL

Currants on a bush
  And figs upon a stem,
And cherries on a bending bough,
  And Ned to gather them.

 ## APRIL

When the cows come home the milk is coming,
Honey's made while the bees are humming;
Duck and drake on the rushy lake,
And the deer live safe in the breezy brake;
And timid, funny, brisk little bunny
Winks his nose and sits all sunny.

 ## APRIL

Where innocent bright-eyed daisies are,
  With blades of grass between,
Each daisy stands up like a star
  Out of a sky of green.

 ## APRIL

Wrens and robins in the hedge,
  Wrens and robins here and there;
Building, perching, pecking, fluttering,
  Everywhere!

# BAA, BAA, BLACK SHEEP

Baa, baa, black sheep, have you any wool?
Yes, sir, yes, sir, three bags full:
One for the master, one for the dame,
And one for the little boy that lives down the lane.

# MARY HAD A LITTLE LAMB

Mary had a little lamb,
Its fleece was white as snow,
And everywhere that Mary went
The lamb was sure to go.

It followed her to school one day,
Which was against the rule;
It made the children laugh and play
To see a lamb in school.

105

# CUSHY COW BONNY

Cushy cow bonny, let down thy milk,
And I will give thee a gown of silk;
A gown of silk and a silver tree,
If thou wilt let down thy milk to me.

# I HAD A LITTLE COW

I had a little cow;
  Hey-diddle, ho-diddle!
I had a little cow, and it had a little calf;
Hey-diddle, ho-diddle; and there's my song half.

I had a little cow;
  Hey-diddle, ho-diddle!
I had a little cow, and I drove it to the stall;
Hey-diddle, ho-diddle; and there's my song all!

# THERE WAS A PIPER, HE'D A COW

There was a piper, he'd a cow,
And he'd no hay to give her;
He took his pipes and played a tune:
"Consider, old cow, consider!"

The cow considered very well,
For she gave the piper a penny,
That he might play the tune again,
Of "Corn rigs are bonnie".

# WAY DOWN YONDER IN THE MAPLE SWAMP

Way down yonder in the maple swamp
The wild geese gather and the ganders honk
The mares kick up and the ponies prance;
The old sow whistles and the little pigs dance.

# BETTY PRINGLE

Betty Pringle had a little pig,
Not very little and not very big;
When he was alive he lived in clover;
But now he's dead, and that's all over.
So Billy Pringle he laid down and cried,
And Betty Pringle she laid down and died;
So there was an end of one, two, and three:
    Billy Pringle he,
    Betty Pringle she,
    And the piggy wiggy.

## 20 APRIL

# THE DAYS ARE CLEAR

The days are clear,
　　Day after day,
When April's here
　　That leads to May,
And June
Must follow soon:
　　Stay, June, stay!–
If only we could stop the moon
And June!

CHRISTINA ROSETTI

# INCEY WINCEY SPIDER

Incey Wincey spider
  Climbing up the spout;
Down came the rain
  And washed the spider out:
Out came the sunshine
  And dried up all the rain;
Incey Wincey spider
  Climbing up again.

# THE HUMBLE-BEE

Two young men were out walking one summer's day and stopped by a tiny stream next to an old ruined house. They were admiring the place, and noticed how the stream turned into a miniature waterfall crossed by narrow blades of grass. One of the men was tired from the walk and the afternoon heat and sat down by the stream. Soon he was fast asleep, and the other sat quietly, watching the view.

Suddenly, a tiny creature, about the size of a humble-bee, flew out of the sleeper's mouth. It landed by the stream and crossed it by walking over some grass stalks which hung over the water at its narrowest point. The creature then approached the ruin and disappeared into one of the cracks in the wall.

The man who saw all this was shocked and decided to wake his friend to see if he was all right. As he shook his companion awake, he was astonished to see the tiny creature emerge from the ruin, fly across the stream and re-enter the sleeper's mouth, just as the young man was waking.

"What's the matter? Are you ill?" asked the watcher.

"I am well," replied the sleeper. "You have just interrupted the most wonderful dream, and I wish you had not woken me

with your shaking. I dreamed that I walked through a vast grassy plain and came to a wide river. I wanted to cross the river to see what was on the other side, and I found a place near a great waterfall where there was a bridge made of silver. I walked over the bridge and on the far bank was a beautiful palace built of stone. When I looked in, the chambers of the palace contained great mounds of gold and jewels. I was look-ing at all these fine things, wondering at the wealth of the person who left them there, and deciding which I would bring away with me. Then suddenly you woke me, and I could bring away none of the riches."

# BOW, WOW, WOW

Bow, wow, wow,
  Whose dog art thou?
"Little Tom Tinker's dog,
  Bow, wow, wow."

# TWO LITTLE DOGS

Two little dogs
  Sat by the fire
Over a fender of coal-dust;
  Said one little dog
  To the other little dog,
If you don't talk, why, I must.

# PUSSY-CAT SITS BY THE FIRE

Pussy-cat sits by the fire.
    How did she come there?
In walks the little dog,
    Says, "Pussy! are you there?
How do you do, Mistress Pussy?
    Mistress Pussy, how d'ye do?"
"I thank you kindly, little dog,
    I fare as well as you!"

# ROBIN AND RICHARD

Robin and Richard were two pretty men;
They laid in bed till the clock struck ten;
Then up starts Robin and looks at the sky,
Oh! brother Richard, the sun's very high:

The bull's in the barn threshing the corn,
The cock's on the dunghill blowing his horn,
The cat's at the fire frying of fish,
The dog's in the pantry breaking his dish.

# LITTLE TOMMY TITTLEMOUSE

Little Tommy Tittlemouse
Lived in a little house;
He caught fishes
In other men's ditches.

 28 APRIL

# SEE-SAW, MARGERY DAW

See-saw, Margery Daw,
Jack shall have a new master;
He shall have but a penny a day,
Because he can't work any faster.

## 29 APRIL

# THREE YOUNG RATS

Three young rats with black felt hats,
Three young ducks with white straw flats,
Three young dogs with curling tails,
Three young cats with demi-veils,
Went out to walk with two young pigs
In satin vests and sorrel wigs;
But suddenly it chanced to rain,
And so they all went home again.

## 30 APRIL

# THE COLD OLD HOUSE

I know a house, and a cold old house,
A cold old house by the sea.
If I were a mouse in that cold old house
What a cold cold mouse I'd be!

# THREE BLIND MICE

Three blind mice, see how they run!
Three blind mice, see how they run!
 They all ran after the farmer's wife,
Who cut off their tails with a carving-knife,
Did ever you hear such a thing in your life,
 As three blind mice.

# BAT, BAT

Bat, Bat, come under my hat,
And I'll give you a slice of bacon,
And when I bake I'll give you a cake,
If I am not mistaken.

 MAY

# HICKORY, DICKORY, DOCK

Hickory, dickory, dock,
The mouse ran up the clock.
The clock struck one,
The mouse ran down,
Hickory, dickory, dock.

# INTERY, MINTERY, CUTERY, CORN

Intery, mintery, cutery, corn,
Apple seed and apple thorn.
Wire, briar, limber, lock,
Three geese in a flock.
One flew east and one flew west;
One flew over the cuckoo's nest.

## 🗓5 MAY

# THE CUCKOO

Cuckoo, Cuckoo,
What do you do?
In April
I open my bill;
In May
I sing night and day;
In June
I change my tune;
In July
Away I fly;
In August
Away I must.

123

 MAY

# THERE WERE TWO BIRDS SAT ON A STONE

There were two birds sat on a stone,
  Fa, la, la, la, lal, de;
One flew away, then there was one,
  Fa, la, la, la, lal, de;
The other flew after, and then there
    was none,
  Fa, la, la, la, lal, de;
And so the poor stone was left all alone,
  Fa, la, la, la, lal, de!

# TWO LITTLE DICKY BIRDS

Two little dicky birds sitting on a wall,
One named Peter, one named Paul.
  Fly away, Peter!
  Fly away, Paul!
    Come back, Peter!
    Come back, Paul!

# THE WORLD

Great, wide, beautiful, wonderful World,
With the wonderful water round you curled,
And the wonderful grass upon your breast–
World, you are beautifully drest.

The wonderful air is over me,
And the wonderful wind is shaking the tree,
It walks on the water, and whirls the mills,
And talks to itself on the tops of the hills.

You friendly Earth, how far do you go,
With the wheatfields that nod and the rivers that flow,
With cities and gardens, and cliffs, and isles,
And people upon you for thousands of miles?

Ah, you are so great, and I am so small,
I tremble to think of you, World, at all;
And yet, when I said my prayers today,
A whisper inside me seemed to say,
"You are more than the Earth, though you are such a dot:
You can love and think, and the Earth cannot."

WILLIAM BRIGHTY RANDS

 MAY

# ANSWER TO A CHILD'S QUESTION

Do you ask what the birds say? The sparrow, the dove,
The linnet and thrush say, "I love and I love!"
In the winter they're silent, the wind is so strong;
What it says I don't know, but it sings a loud song.
But green leaves, and blossoms, and sunny warm weather,
And singing and loving-all come back together.
But the lark is so brimful of gladness and love,
The green fields below him, the blue sky above,
That he sings, and he sings, and for ever sings he,
"I love my Love, and my Love loves me."

SAMUEL TAYLOR COLERIDGE

# A WHITE HEN

A white hen sitting
  On white eggs three:
Next, three speckled chickens
  As plump as plump can be.

An owl and a hawk
  And a bat come to see;
But chicks beneath their mother's wing
  Squat safe as safe can be.

# THE GRAND OLD DUKE OF YORK

The grand old Duke of York,
    He had ten thousand men;
He marched them up to the top of the hill,
    And he marched them down again!
And when they were up they were up,
    And when they were down they were down;
And when they were only halfway up,
    They were neither up nor down.

## 12 MAY

# HUSH-A-BYE, BABY

Hush-a-bye, baby, on the tree top,
When the wind blows the cradle will rock;
When the bough breaks the cradle will fall,
Down will come baby, cradle and all.

 MAY

# ALL THE PRETTY LITTLE HORSES

Hush-a-bye, don't you cry,
Go to sleepy little baby.
When you wake
You shall have
All the pretty little horses.
Blacks and bays,
Dapples and greys,
Coach and six white horses.

Hush-a-bye, don't you cry,
Go to sleepy little baby.
When you wake
You shall have cake
And all the pretty little horses.

# ROCK-A-BYE, BABY

Rock-a-bye, baby, thy cradle is green;
Father's a nobleman, Mother's a queen,
And Betty's a lady, and wears a gold ring,
And Johnny's a drummer, and drums for the King.

# BYE, BABY BUNTING

Bye, baby bunting,
Father's gone a-hunting,
To fetch a little rabbit-skin
To wrap his baby bunting in.

 MAY

# COME TO BED, SAYS SLEEPY-HEAD

Come to bed,
Says Sleepy-head;
 "Tarry a while," says Slow;
"Put on the pot,"
Says Greedy-gut,
 "Let's sup before we go."

# DIDDLE, DIDDLE, DUMPLING

Diddle, diddle, dumpling, my son John
Went to bed with his trousers on;
One shoe off, the other shoe on,
Diddle, diddle, dumpling, my son John.

# LITTLE BOY BLUE

Little Boy Blue,
  Come blow your horn,
The sheep's in the meadow,
  The cow's in the corn.

Where is the boy
  Who looks after the sheep?
He's under a haycock
  Fast asleep.
Will you wake him?
  No, not I,
For if I do,
  He's sure to cry.

MAY

# THERE WAS A LITTLE BOY

There was a little boy went into a barn,
And lay down on some hay;
An owl came out and flew about,
And the little boy ran away.

##  20 MAY

A frisky lamb
And a frisky child
Playing their pranks
  In a cowslip meadow:
The sky all blue
And the air all mild
And the fields all sun
  And the lanes half shadow.

##  21 MAY

On the grassy banks
Lambkins at their pranks;
Woolly sisters, woolly brothers,
  Jumping off their feet,
While their woolly mothers
  Watch by them and bleat.

##  22 MAY

O wind, why do you never rest,
Wandering, whistling to and fro,
Bringing rain out of the west,
  From the dim north bringing snow?

138

 ## MAY

The wind has such a rainy sound
  Moaning through the town,
The sea has such a windy sound,–
  Will the ships go down?

The apples in the orchard
  Tumble from their tree,–
Oh will the ships go down, go down,
  In the windy sea?

 ## MAY

Motherless baby and babyless mother,
Bring them together to love one another.

 ## MAY

Swift and sure the swallow,
  Slow and sure the snail:
Slow and sure may miss his way,
  Swift and sure may fail.

# A SWARM OF BEES IN MAY

A swarm of bees in May
Is worth a load of hay;
A swarm of bees in June
Is worth a silver spoon;
A swarm of bees in July
Is not worth a fly.

 MAY

# WHAT DO THE STARS DO?

What do the stars do
  Up in the sky,
Higher than the wind can blow,
  Or the clouds can fly?

Each star in its own glory
  Circles, circles still;
As it was lit to shine and set,
  And do its Maker's will.

 MAY

# THE LILY HAS AN AIR

The lily has an air,
  And the snowdrop a grace,
And the sweetpea a way,
  And the heartsease a face,–
Yet there's nothing like the rose
  When she blows.

# PEASE-PUDDING HOT

Pease-pudding hot,
  Pease-pudding cold,
Pease-pudding in the pot,
  Nine days old.
Some like it hot,
  Some like it cold,
Some like it in the pot,
  Nine days old.

MAY

# THE MAN IN THE MOON

The man in the moon,
 Came tumbling down,
And asked his way to Norwich.
 He went by the south,
 And burnt his mouth
With supping cold pease-porridge.

 MAY

# HIGGLETY, PIGGLETY, POP!

Higglety, pigglety, pop!
The dog has eaten the mop;
  The pig's in a hurry,
  The cat's in a flurry,
Higglety, pigglety, pop!

 JUNE

# WE'RE ALL IN THE DUMPS

We're all in the dumps,
For diamonds and trumps,
The kittens are gone to St. Paul's,
The babies are bit,
The moon's in a fit,
And the houses are built without walls.

 JUNE

# RING-A-RING O' ROSES

Ring-a ring o' roses
A pocket full of posies,
A-tishoo! A-tishoo!
We all fall down.

145

# THE MILLER OF DEE

There was a jolly miller
  Lived on the river Dee:
He worked and sung from morn till night,
  No lark so blithe as he;
And this the burden of his song
  For ever used to be–
I jump mejerrime jee!
  I care for nobody–no! not I,
Since nobody cares for me.

146

## 4 JUNE

# AS I WAS GOING ALONG

As I was going along, long, long,
A singing a comical song, song, song,
The lane that I went was so long, long, long,
And the song that I sung was as long, long, long,
And so I went singing along.

 JUNE

# OVER THE HILLS AND FAR AWAY

When I was young and had no sense
I bought a fiddle for eighteenpence,
And the only tune that I could play
Was "Over the Hills and Far Away".

 JUNE

# HEY, DIDDLE, DIDDLE

Hey, diddle, diddle, the cat and the fiddle,
The cow jumped over the moon;
The little dog laughed to see such sport,
And the dish ran away with the spoon!

# GOOSEY, GOOSEY, GANDER

Goosey, goosey, gander,
  Whither shall I wander,
Upstairs, and downstairs,
  And in my lady's chamber.
There I met an old man,
  Who would not say his prayers,
I took him by his left leg
  And threw him down the stairs.

# DAFFY-DOWN-DILLY

Daffy-
   Down-
Dilly
   has come
up to
   town

In a
   yellow
petticoat
   and a
green
   gown.

 JUNE

# FROM WIBBLETON TO WOBBLETON

From Wibbleton to Wobbleton
  is fifteen miles,
From Wobbleton to Wibbleton
  is fifteen miles,
From Wibbleton to Wobbleton,
From Wobbleton to Wibbleton,
From Wibbleton to Wobbleton
  is fifteen miles.

152

 JUNE

# SEE-SAW, SACRADOWN

See-saw, Sacradown,
Which is the way to London Town?
One foot up and one foot down,
That's the way to London Town.

153

⟨11⟩ JUNE

# HUMPTY DUMPTY

Humpty Dumpty sat on a wall,
Humpty Dumpty had a great fall;
All the king's horses and all the king's men
Couldn't put Humpty together again.

# TWEEDLE-DUM AND TWEEDLE-DEE

Tweedle-dum and Tweedle-dee
  Agreed to have a battle,
For Tweedle-dum said Tweedle-dee
  Had spoiled his nice new rattle.
Just then flew down a monstrous crow,
  As big as a tar-barrel,
Which frightened both the heroes so,
  They quite forgot their quarrel.

# ROBIN THE BOBBIN

Robin the Bobbin, the big-bellied Ben,
He ate more meat than fourscore men;
He ate a cow, he ate a calf,
He ate a butcher and a half;
He ate a church, he ate a steeple,
He ate the priest and all the people!
    A cow and a calf,
    An ox and a half,
    A church and a steeple,
    And all the good people,
And yet he complained that his stomach wasn't full.

156

# HECTOR PROTECTOR

Hector Protector was dressed all in green;
Hector Protector was sent to the Queen.
The Queen did not like him,
Nor more did the King;
So Hector Protector was sent back again.

# FIVE LITTLE MONKEYS

Five little monkeys walked along the shore;
One went a-sailing,
Then there were four.
Four little monkeys climbed up a tree;
One of them tumbled down,
Then there were three.
Three little monkeys found a pot of glue;
One got stuck in it,
Then there were two.
Two little monkeys found a currant bun;
One ran away with it,
Then there was one.
One little monkey cried all afternoon,
So they put him in an aeroplane
And sent him to the moon.

# THREE CHILDREN

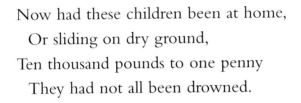

Three children sliding on the ice
   Upon a summer's day,
As it fell out, they all fell in,
   The rest they ran away.

Now had these children been at home,
   Or sliding on dry ground,
Ten thousand pounds to one penny
   They had not all been drowned.

You parents all that children have,
   And you that have got none,
If you would have them safe abroad,
   Pray keep them safe at home.

 JUNE

# A RARE QUARRY

Two friends were out hunting otters and they walked beside a stream, looking at the banks for holes where the creatures might be hiding. Suddenly, one of them saw a flash of red. The creature moved quickly, darting along the bank and vanishing into a hole near a tree.

One friend turned to the other: "What was that? It was too large for a squirrel, too small for a fox. Could it be a rare, red-furred otter?"

The two men had never seen such an otter before, but could not think what other sort of creature it might be, so decided to try to catch it. They looked carefully at the burrow and saw that it had two entrances, one on either side of the tree. "We'll need a sack," said the first man, and he ran off to a nearby farm to borrow one.

When he returned, he held the sack over one end of the burrow, while his friend stood at the other end and made a noise to frighten the creature out. Sure enough, there was a mighty plop as the creature jumped into the sack. Holding the end closed, the two men made off for home, very pleased with their rare quarry.

The pair walked home across the fields, and had not gone very far when they were amazed to hear a tiny voice inside the sack calling "I hear my mother calling me. I hear my mother calling me." The men dropped the sack in astonishment and watched as a tiny figure climbed out. On his head was a red hat, and he wore trousers and jacket and shoes that were also bright red. As he ran off towards the cover of some low bushes, again he looked like a streak of red, and the men saw how easy it had been to mistake him for an animal.

Looking at each other in alarm, the two hunters ran off towards home. They never hunted for otters again on that stretch of the river.

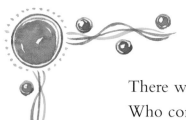

 ## 18 JUNE

There was an old man with an owl,
Who continued to bother and howl;
He sat on a rail, and imbibed bitter ale,
Which refreshed that old man and his owl.

 ## 19 JUNE

The rose with such a bonny blush,
What has the rose to blush about?
If it's the sun that makes her flush,
What's in the sun to flush about?

 ## 20 JUNE

There was an old man in a tree,
Whose whiskers were lovely to see;
But the birds of the air plucked them perfectly bare,
To make themselves nests in that tree.

 ## 21 JUNE

Old woman, old woman, shall we go a-shearing?
Speak a little louder sir, I'm very hard of hearing.
Old woman, old woman, shall I love you dearly?
Thank you, kind sir, I hear you very clearly.

##  JUNE

There was an old man, on whose nose,
Most birds of the air could repose;
But they all flew away, at the closing of day,
Which relieved that old man and his nose.

##  JUNE

Wun-wun was a racehorse,
Tu-tu was one too.
Wun-wun won one race,
Tu-tu won one too.

## JUNE

The cat sat asleep by the side of the fire,
The mistress snored loud as a pig.
Jack took up his fiddle, by Jenny's desire,
And struck up a bit of a jig.

## JUNE

There was an old person of Brigg,
Who purchased no end of a wig;
So that only his nose, and the end of his toes,
Could be seen when he walked about Brigg.

# A CAT CAME FIDDLING OUT OF A BARN

A cat came fiddling out of a barn,
With a pair of bagpipes under her arm;
She could sing nothing but fiddle cum fee,
The mouse has married the humble-bee.
Pipe, cat-dance, mouse,
We'll have a wedding at our good house.

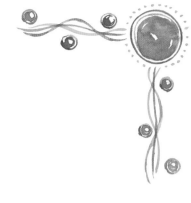

### 🗓 27 JUNE

# DING, DONG, BELL

Ding, dong, bell,
Pussy's in the well.
  Who put her in?
  Little Tommy Green.
Who pulled her out?
Little Tommy Stout.
  What a naughty boy was that,
  To try and drown poor pussy cat.
Who never did him any harm,
And killed the mice in his Father's barn.

# FOLLOW MY BANGALOREY MAN

Follow my Bangalorey Man,
Follow my Bangalorey Man;
I'll do all that ever I can
To follow my Bangalorey Man.
We'll borrow a horse, and steal a gig,
And round the world we'll do a jig,
And I'll do all that ever I can
To follow my Bangalorey Man!

 JUNE

# ANNA MARIA

Anna Maria she sat on the fire;
The fire was too hot, she sat on the pot;
The pot was too round, she sat on the ground;
The ground was too flat, she sat on the cat;
The cat ran away with Maria on her back.

167

# HANDY SPANDY, JACK-A-DANDY

Handy Spandy, Jack-a-dandy
Loved plum-cake and sugar-candy;
He bought some at a grocer's shop,
And out he came, hop, hop, hop.

168

# YANKEE DOODLE

Yankee Doodle went to town,
Riding on a pony;
He stuck a feather in his hat,
And called it macaroni.
    Yankee Doodle fa, so, la,
    Yankee Doodle dandy,
    Yankee Doodle fa, so, la,
    Buttermilk and brandy.

Yankee Doodle went to town
To buy a pair of trousers,
He swore he could not see the town
For so many houses.
    Yankee Doodle fa, so, la,
    Yankee Doodle dandy,
    Yankee Doodle fa, so, la,
    Buttermilk and brandy.

## 2 JULY

# HARK! HARK!

Hark, hark,
The dogs do bark,
Beggars are coming to town:
Some in rags,
Some in tags,
And some in velvet gowns.

# 3 JULY

# IF WISHES WERE HORSES

If wishes were horses,
   Beggars would ride;
If turnips were watches,
   I'd wear one by my side.

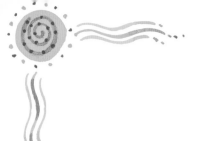

 JULY

# THE LOST KINGDOM

In former times, the best land in Wales lay towards the West. The fertile plains and lush grasslands were fine country for farming, and all who worked these fields grew rich. But there was one problem with the country in the West. The ground lay so low that it was often flooded by the sea. So the kings of the West built a great wall, with strong sluice gates, to hold back the sea. For many years the people of the West enjoyed a life without floods, and they became the envy of all Wales.

One of the greatest of all the western kings was Gwyddno. Sixteen beautiful cities grew up in his kingdom while he reigned, and the lands of the West became more prosperous

than before. After the king, the most important person in the kingdom of the West was a man called Seithennin, whom Gwyddno appointed as the keeper of the sluices. Whenever a storm brewed, and the sea threatened to overwhelm the kingdom, Seithennin would close the great sluice gates, and the lands of the West would be safe.

Seithennin was a big, strong man, chosen because he could easily turn the handles to close the heavy oak sluice gates. But there was a problem. Seithennin was a drunkard. Sometimes, when he had had too much to drink, he would be late to close the gates, and there would be some slight flooding. But the kingdom would recover, and no great harm was done.

One day, King Gwyddno ordered a great banquet in his hall. All the lords and ladies of the kingdom were there, as well as other men of importance such as Seithennin. The banquet went on long into the night, and the sluice-keeper got more

and more drunk. There was singing and harping, and everyone was enjoying themselves to the full. But because of all the noise of the revelling, no-one could hear that a great storm was brewing up outside. Even when people did start to notice, they assumed that Seithennin had closed the sluice gates and that they would be safe from flooding, as they had been for years now. But no one saw that the sluice-keeper, who had drunk more than anyone else at the banquet, was fast asleep.

Outside, the waters of the sea were pouring through the sluice gates. Soon the fields were flooded and the streets of the towns were awash. But still the banquet went on, until the flood waters poured through the doors of Gwyddno's hall. There had been floods in this part of Wales in earlier years, before the sea wall was built. Then people had lost their lives and good farm land had been spoiled.

But this time it was worse. The water poured in with such speed that it was unstoppable. Men, women, and children, lords and servants alike, were swept under the flood. Even those who knew the sea, including many fishermen who were excellent swimmers, lost their lives. Sheep and cattle went the same way. Soon the whole great kingdom of the West, every field and every town, was deep under the water. And all were drowned apart from one man, the poet Taliesin, who survived to tell the tale. They say that the sigh that Gwyddno let out as he was lost

under the waves was the saddest sound ever heard.

The sea now covers Gwyddno's former kingdom, in the place now called Cardigan Bay. Occasionally, at low tide, wooden posts and fragments of stone wall are revealed among the sand, and men say that these are the last remaining parts of one of Gwyddno's cities. Sailors and fishermen who cross the bay say that they can sometimes hear the bells of the sixteen cities, sounding beneath the waves, reminding them of the terrible power of the sea. Some even say that on a quiet, still day they can hear the echoing sound of Gwyddno's final sigh.

# GIRLS AND BOYS COME OUT TO PLAY

Girls and boys, come out to play;
The moon doth shine as bright as day;
Leave your supper, and leave your sleep,
And come with your playfellows into the street.
Come with a whoop, come with a call,
Come with a good will or not at all.
Up the ladder and down the wall,
A halfpenny roll will serve us all.
You find milk, and I'll find flour,
And we'll have a pudding in half-an-hour.

Georgie, Porgie, pudding and pie,
Kissed the girls and made them cry;
When the boys came out to play
Georgie Porgie ran away.

 JULY

I scream, you scream,
We all scream for ice cream!

JULY

# CLUCK! CLUCK!

Cluck! cluck! the nursing hen
Summons her folk,–
Ducklings all downy soft,
Yellow as yolk.

Cluck! cluck! the mother hen
Summons her chickens
To peck the dainty bits
Found in her pickings.

CHRISTINA ROSSETTI

# A RACE

A daisy and a buttercup
Agreed to have a race,
A squirrel was to be the judge
A mile off from the place.

The squirrel waited patiently
Until the day was done.
Perhaps he is there waiting still,
You see, they couldn't run.

MARY LOUISA MOLESWORTH

# THE MAN IN THE WILDERNESS

The man in the Wilderness asked me,
How many strawberries grew in the sea?
I answered him as I thought good,
As many red herrings as grew in the wood.

## 11 JULY

# A PEANUT SAT ON THE RAILROAD TRACK

A peanut sat on the railroad track,
His heart was all a-flutter;
Along came a train–the 9:15–
Toot, toot, peanut butter!

180

# THE QUEEN OF HEARTS

The Queen of Hearts, she made some tarts,
  All on a summer's day;
The Knave of Hearts, he stole the tarts,
  And took them clean away.

The King of Hearts called for the tarts,
  And beat the Knave full sore;
The Knave of Hearts brought back the tarts,
  And vowed he'd steal no more.

 JULY

# IF ALL THE WORLD WAS APPLE PIE

If all the world was apple pie,
  And all the sea was ink,
And all the trees were bread and cheese,
  What should we have for drink?

# FOR WANT OF A NAIL

For want of a nail, the shoe was lost;
For want of the shoe, the horse was lost;
For want of the horse, the rider was lost;
For want of the rider, the battle was lost;
For want of the battle, the kingdom was lost;
And all from the want of a horseshoe nail.

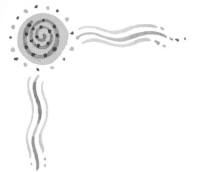

 JULY

# THE FENODEREE

On the Isle of Man lived a fairy who had been sent out of fairyland because he had had a passion for a mortal girl. The fairy folk found out about his love for the girl when he was absent from one of their gatherings. They found him dancing with his love in the merry Glen of Rushen. When the other fairies heard what he was doing, they cast a spell, forcing him to live for ever on the Isle of Man, and making him ugly and hairy. This is why people called him the Fenoderee, which means "hairy one" in the Manx language.

Although his appearance frightened people when they saw him, the Fenoderee was usually kind to humans, for he never forgot the girl he loved, and wanted to do what he could for her people. Sometimes he even helped people with their work, and used what was left of his fairy magic to carry out tasks which would have been exhausting for the strongest of men.

One thing the Fenoderee liked to do was to help the farmers in their fields. On one occasion he mowed a meadow for a farmer. But instead of being grateful, the farmer complained that the Fenoderee had not cut the grass short enough.

The Fenoderee was still sad at losing his mortal love, and angry that the farmer was so ungrateful, so next year at mowing time, he let the farmer do the job himself.

As the farmer walked along, swishing his scythe from side to side, the Fenoderee crept behind him, cutting up roots, and getting so close to the farmer that the man risked having his feet cut off.

When the farmer told this story, people knew that they should be grateful when the Fenoderee helped them with their work. So the custom arose of leaving the creature little gifts when he had been especially helpful.

185

On one occasion, a man was building himself a new house of stone. He found the stone he wanted on the cliffs by the beach, and paid some of the men of the parish to help him quarry it. There was one large block of fine marble which he especially wanted, but no matter how hard they tried, the block was too heavy to be moved, even if all the men of the parish tried to shift it.

Next day they were surprised to see that not only had the huge block of marble been carried to the building site, but all the other stone that the builder needed had been moved too.

At first, everyone wondered how the stone could have got there. But then someone said, "It must have been the Fenoderee who was working for us in the night." The builder

saw that this must be true, and thought that he should give the Fenoderee a handsome reward.

So he took some clothes of the right size for the creature, and left them in one of the places where he was sometimes seen. That night, the Fenoderee appeared and found the clothes. Those who watched him were surprised at his sadness as he lifted each item up in turn and said these words:

Cap for the head, alas, poor head!

Coat for the back, alas, poor back!

Breeches for the breech, alas, poor breech!

If these all be thine, thine cannot be the merry glen of Rushen. With these words, the Fenoderee walked away, and has never been seen since in that neighbourhood.

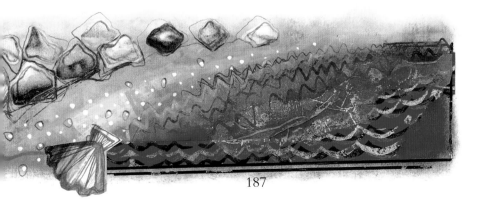

# CALICO PIE

Calico Pie,
The little Birds fly
Down to the calico tree,
Their wings were blue,
And they sang "Tilly-loo!"
Till away they flew–
And they never came back to me!
They never came back!
They never came back!
They never came back to me!

Calico Jam,
The little Fish swam,
Over the syllabub sea,
He took off his hat,
To the Sole and the Sprat,
And the Willeby-wat,–
But he never came back to me!
He never came back!
He never came back!
He never came back to me!

Calico Ban,
The little Mice ran,
To be ready in time for tea,
Flippity flup,
They drank it all up,
And danced in the cup,–
But they never came back to me!
They never came back!
They never came back!
They never came back to me!

Calico Drum,
The Grasshoppers come,
The Butterfly, Beetle, and Bee,
Over the ground,
Around and round,
With a hop and a bound,–
But they never came back!
They never came back!
They never came back!
They never came back to me!

EDWARD LEAR

# DONKEY RIDING

Were you ever in Quebec,
Stowing timbers on a deck,
Where there's a king in his golden crown
  Riding on a donkey?

Hey ho, and away we go,
  Donkey riding, donkey riding,
Hey ho, and away we go,
  Riding on a donkey.

Were you ever in Cardiff Bay,
Where the folks all shout, Hooray!
Here comes John with his three months' pay,
  Riding on a donkey?

Hey ho, and away we go,
  Donkey riding, donkey riding,
Hey ho, and away we go,
  Riding on a donkey.

Were you ever off Cape Horn,
Where it's always fine and warm?
See the lion and the unicorn
  Riding on a donkey.

Hey ho, and away we go,
  Donkey riding, donkey riding,
Hey ho, and away we go,
  Riding on a donkey.

ANONYMOUS
ENGLISH SEA SHANTY

191

# THE BUTTERFLY'S BALL

Come take up your hats, and away let us haste,
To the Butterfly's Ball, and the Grasshopper's Feast.
The trumpeter Gadfly has summoned the crew,
And the revels are now only waiting for you.

On the smooth-shaven grass by the side of a wood,
Beneath a broad oak which for ages has stood,
See the children of earth and the tenants of air,
For an evening's amusement together repair.

And there came the Beetle, so blind and so black,
Who carried the Emmet, his friend, on his back.
And there came the Gnat, and the Dragonfly too,
And all their relations, green, orange, and blue.

And there came the Moth, with her plumage of down,
And the Hornet, with jacket of yellow and brown;
Who with him the Wasp, his companion, did bring,
But they promised that evening, to lay by their sting.

192

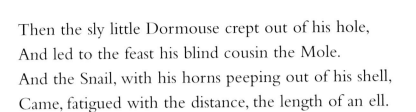

Then the sly little Dormouse crept out of his hole,
And led to the feast his blind cousin the Mole.
And the Snail, with his horns peeping out of his shell,
Came, fatigued with the distance, the length of an ell.

A mushroom their table, and on it was laid
A water-dock leaf, which a tablecloth made.
The viands were various, to each of their taste,
And the Bee brought the honey to sweeten the feast.

With steps most majestic the Snail did advance,
And he promised the gazers a minuet to dance;
But they all laughed so loud that he drew in his head,
And went in his own little chamber to bed.

Then, as evening gave way to the shadows of night,
Their watchman, the Glow-worm, came out with his light.
So home let us hasten, while yet we can see;
For no watchman is waiting for you and for me.

WILLIAM ROSCOE

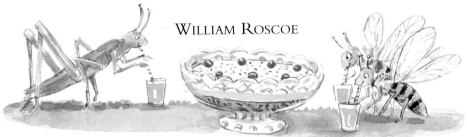

# THE STORY OF THE LITTLE BIRD

Once long ago in a monastery in Ireland there lived a holy man. He was walking one day in the garden of his monastery, when he decided to kneel down and pray, to give thanks to God for the beauty of all the flowers and plants and herbs around him. As he did so, he heard a small bird singing, and never before had he heard any song as sweet. When his prayers were finished, the monk stood up and listened to the bird, and

when the creature flew away from the garden, singing as it went, he followed it.

In a while they came to a small grove of trees outside the monastery grounds, and there the bird continued its song. As the bird hopped from tree to tree, still singing all the while, the monk carried on following the little creature, until they had gone a great distance. The more the bird sang, the more the monk was enchanted by the music it made.

Eventually, the two had travelled far away from the monastery, and the monk realised that it would soon be night-time. So reluctantly, he left the bird behind and retraced his steps, arriving back home as the sun was going down in the west. As the sun set, it lit up the sky with all the colours of the rainbow, and the monk thought that the sight was almost as beautiful and heavenly as the song of the little bird he had been listening to all afternoon long.

But the glorious sunset was not the only sight that surprised the monk. As he entered the abbey gates, everything around him seemed changed from before. In the garden grew different plants, in the courtyard the brothers had different faces, and even the abbey buildings seemed to have altered. He knew he was in the right place, yet how could all these changes have taken place in a single afternoon?

The holy man walked across the courtyard and greeted the

first monk he saw. "Brother, how is it that our abbey has changed so much since this morning? There are fresh plants in the garden, new faces amongst the brothers, and even the stones of the church seem different."

The second monk looked at the holy man carefully. "Why do you ask these questions, brother? There have been no changes. Our church and gardens have not altered since morning, and we have no new brothers here – except for yourself, for though you wear the habit of our order, I have not seen you before." And the two monks looked at each other in wonder. Neither could understand what had happened.

When he saw that the

brother was puzzled, the holy man started to tell his story. He told his companion how he had gone to walk in the monastery garden, how he had heard the little bird, and how he had followed the creature far into the countryside to listen to its song.

As the holy man spoke, the expression on the second monk's face turned from puzzlement to surprise. He said, "There is a story in our order about a brother like you who went missing one day after a bird was heard singing. He never returned to the abbey, and no one knew what befell him, and all this happened two hundred years ago."

The holy man looked at his companion and replied, "That is indeed my story. The time of my death has finally arrived. Praised be the Lord for his mercies to me." And the holy man begged the second monk to take his confession and give him absolution, for the hour of his death was near. All this was done, the holy man died before midnight, and he was buried with great solemnity in the abbey church.

Ever since, the monks of the abbey have told this story. They say that the little bird was an angel of the Lord, and that this was God's way of taking the soul of a man who was known for his holiness and his love of the beauties of nature.

# SIMPLE GIFTS

'Tis the gift to be simple,
'Tis the gift to be free,
'Tis the gift to come down
Where we ought to be,
And when we find ourselves
In the place just right,
'Twill be in the valley
Of love and delight.
When true simplicity is gained
To bow and to bend
We sha'n't be ashamed,
To turn, turn will be our delight,
Till by turning, turning
We come round right.

ANONYMOUS
AMERICAN, SHAKER SONG

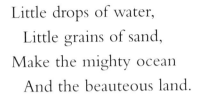 JULY

# LITTLE THINGS

Little drops of water,
 Little grains of sand,
Make the mighty ocean
 And the beauteous land.

And the little moments,
 Humble though they be,
Make the mighty ages
 Of eternity.

So our little errors
 Lead the soul away,
From the paths of virtue
 Into sin to stray.

Little deeds of kindness,
 Little words of love,
Make our earth an Eden,
 Like the heaven above.

JULIA A. CARNEY

199

# WHOLE DUTY OF CHILDREN

A child should always say what's true,
And speak when he is spoken to,
And behave mannerly at table:
At least as far as he is able.

ROBERT LOUIS STEVENSON

# DON'T-CARE

Don't-care didn't care;
  Don't-care was wild.
Don't-care stole plum and pear
  Like any beggar's child.

Don't-care was made to care,
  Don't-care was hung:
Don't-care was put in the pot
  And boiled till he was done.

ANONYMOUS
ENGLISH

## 24 JULY

# THE WIND

Who has seen the wind?
  Neither I nor you;
But when the leaves hang trembling
  The wind is passing through.

Who has seen the wind?
  Neither you nor I;
But when the trees bow down their heads
  The wind is passing by.

CHRISTINA ROSSETTI

# FROM A RAILWAY CARRIAGE

Faster than fairies, faster than witches,
Bridges and houses, hedges and ditches;
And charging along like troops in a battle,
All through the meadows the horses and cattle:
All of the sights of the hill and the plain
Fly as thick as driving rain;
And ever again, in the wink of an eye,
Painted stations whistle by.

Here is a child who clambers and scrambles,
All by himself and gathering brambles;
Here is a tramp who stands and gazes;
And there is the green for stringing the daisies!
Here is a cart run away in the road
Lumping along with man and load;
And here is a mill, and there is a river:
Each a glimpse and gone for ever!

ROBERT LOUIS STEVENSON

203

# A BABY-SERMON

The lightning and thunder
They go and they come;
But the stars and the stillness
Are always at home.

GEORGE MACDONALD

# WAGTAIL AND BABY

A baby watched a ford, whereto
  A wagtail came for drinking;
A blaring bull went wading through,
  The wagtail showed no shrinking.

A stallion splashed his way across,
  The birdie nearly sinking;
He gave his plumes a twitch and toss,
  And held his own unblinking.

Next saw the baby round the spot
  A mongrel slowing slinking;
The wagtail gazed, but faltered not
  In dip and sip and prinking.

A perfect gentleman then neared;
  The wagtail, in a winking,
With terror rose and disappeared;
  The baby fell a-thinking.

THOMAS HARDY

205

28 JULY

# ROUND AND ROUND THE GARDEN

Round and round the garden
Like a teddy bear;
One step, two step,
Tickle you under there!

 29 JULY

# THIS LITTLE PIGGY

This little piggy went to market,
This little piggy stayed at home,
This little piggy had roast beef,
This little piggy had none,
And this little piggy cried, *Wee-wee-wee-wee-wee,*
  All the way home.

## 30 JULY

# MY MOTHER AND YOUR MOTHER

My mother and your mother
  Went over the way;
Said my mother to your mother,
  It's chop-a-nose day!

JULY

# A FACE GAME

Here sits the Lord Mayor;          *Forehead*

   Here sit his two men;          *Eyes*

Here sits the cock;          *Right cheek*

   Here sits the hen;          *Left cheek*

Here sit the little chickens;          *Tip of nose*

   Here they run in,          *Mouth*

Chinchopper, chinchopper,

   Chinchopper, chin!          *Chuck the chin*

# THE FLY

Little Fly,
Thy summer's play
My thoughtless hand
Has brushed away.

Am not I
A fly like thee?
Or art not thou
A man like me?

For I dance,
And drink, and sing,
Till some blind hand
Shall brush my wing.

If thought is life
And strength and breath,
And the want
Of thought is death;

Them am I
A happy fly,
If I live
Or if I die.

WILLIAM BLAKE

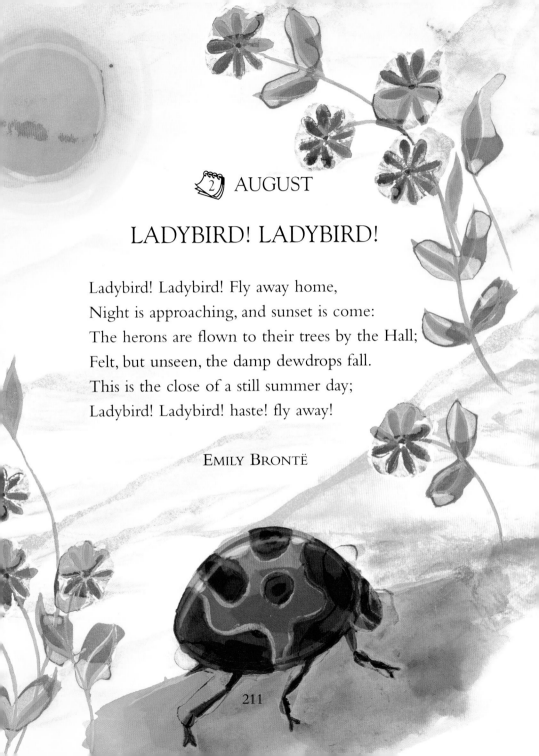

## 2 AUGUST

# LADYBIRD! LADYBIRD!

Ladybird! Ladybird! Fly away home,
Night is approaching, and sunset is come:
The herons are flown to their trees by the Hall;
Felt, but unseen, the damp dewdrops fall.
This is the close of a still summer day;
Ladybird! Ladybird! haste! fly away!

EMILY BRONTË

# 3 AUGUST

## TO MARKET, TO MARKET

To market, to market,
To buy a plum bun;
Home again, come again,
Market is done.

# 4 AUGUST

## TO MARKET, TO MARKET, TO BUY A FAT PIG

To market, to market, to buy a fat pig,
Home again, home again, dancing a jig;
Ride to the market to buy a fat hog,
Home again, home again, jiggety-jog.

# THIS IS THE WAY THE LADIES RIDE

This is the way the ladies ride:
  Tri, tre, tre, tree,
  Tri, tre, tre, tree!
This is the way the ladies ride:
  Tri, tre, tre, tre, tri-tre-tre-tree!

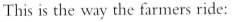

This is the way the gentlemen ride:
  Gallop-a-trot,
  Gallop-a-trot!
This is the way the gentlemen ride:
  Gallop-a-gallop-a-trot!

This is the way the farmers ride:
  Hobbledy-hoy,
  Hobbledy-hoy!
This is the way the farmers ride:
  Hobbledy hobbledy-hoy!

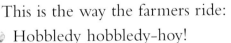

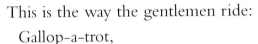

# LEG OVER LEG

Leg over leg,
   As the dog went to Dover;
When he came to a stile,
   Jump he went over.

6 AUGUST

# MICHAEL FINNEGAN

There was an old man called Michael Finnegan
He grew whiskers on his chinnegan
The wind came out and blew them in again
Poor old Michael Finnegan. *Begin again...*

# RIDE A COCK-HORSE

Ride a cock-horse to Banbury Cross,
   To see a fine lady ride on a white horse,
Rings on her fingers and bells on her toes,
   She shall have music wherever she goes.

215

# I AM A GOLD LOCK

### FOR TWO VOICES

I am a gold lock.

*I am a gold key.*

I am a silver lock.

*I am a silver key.*

I am a brass lock.

*I am a brass key.*

I am a lead lock.

*I am a lead key.*

I am a monk lock.

*I am a monk key!*

# AUGUST

## I WENT UP ONE PAIR OF STAIRS

### FOR TWO VOICES

I went up one pair of stairs.
*Just like me.*
I went up two pair of stairs.
*Just like me.*
I went into a room.
*Just like me.*
I looked out of a window.
*Just like me.*
And there I saw a monkey.
*Just like me.*

 AUGUST

# THE DARK WOOD

In the dark, dark wood, there was
  a dark, dark house,
And in that dark, dark house, there was
  a dark, dark room,
And in that dark, dark room, there was
  a dark, dark cupboard,
And in that dark, dark cupboard, there was
  a dark, dark shelf,
And on that dark, dark shelf, there was
  a dark, dark box,
And in that dark, dark box, there was a
GHOST!

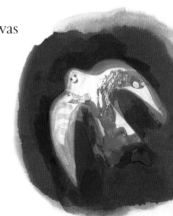

## 12 AUGUST

# I MET A MAN

As I was going up the stair
I met a man who wasn't there.
He wasn't there again today–
Oh! how I wish he'd go away!

![calendar] 13 AUGUST

# ADAM AND EVE AND PINCHME

Adam and Eve and Pinchme
Went down to the river to bathe.
Adam and Eve were drowned–
Who do you think was saved?

![calendar] 14 AUGUST

# ME, MYSELF, AND I

Me, myself, and I–
We went to the kitchen and ate a pie.
Then my mother she came in
And chased us out with a rolling pin.

# PETER PIPER

Peter Piper picked a peck of pickled pepper;
A peck of pickled pepper Peter Piper picked;
If Peter Piper picked a peck of pickled pepper,
Where's the peck of pickled pepper Peter Piper picked?

 AUGUST

# THE SHORTEST TONGUE-TWISTER

Peggy Babcock

# THE WELL AT THE WORLD'S END

There was once a king, a widower, and he had a daughter who was beautiful and good-natured. The king married a queen, who was a widow, and she had a daughter who was as ugly and ill-natured as the king's daughter was fair and good. The queen detested the king's daughter, for no one would notice her own girl while this paragon was beside her, so she made a plan. She sent the king's daughter to the well at the world's end, with a bottle to get some water, thinking she would never come back.

The girl walked far and was beginning to tire when she came upon a pony tethered by the roadside. The pony looked at the girl and spoke: "Ride me, ride me, fair princess."

"Yes, I will ride you," replied the girl, and the pony carried her over a moor covered with prickly gorse and brambles.

Far she rode, and finally she came to the well at the world's end. She took her bottle and lowered it into the well, but the well was too deep and she could not fill the bottle. Then three old men came up to her, saying, "Wash us, wash us, fair maid, and dry us with your linen apron."

So she washed the men and in return they lowered her bottle into the well and filled it with water.

When they had finished, the three men looked at the girl and spoke her future. "If she was fair before, she will be ten times more beautiful," said the first.

"A diamond and a ruby and a pearl shall drop from her mouth every time she speaks," predicted the second.

"Gold and silver shall come from her hair when she combs it," said the third.

The king's daughter returned to court, and to everyone's amazement, these predictions came true.

All were happy with the girl's good fortune, except for the

223

queen and her daughter. The queen decided that she would send her own daughter to the well at the world's end, to get her the same gifts. After travelling far, the girl came to the pony, as the king's daughter had done before her. By now, the beast was tethered once more. But when the creature asked her to ride it, the queen's daughter replied, "Don't you see I am a queen's daughter? I will not ride you, you filthy beast."

The proud girl walked on, and she soon came to the moor covered with gorse and brambles. It was hard going for the girl, and the thorns cut her feet badly. Soon she could hardly walk with the pain.

After a long and painful walk across the moor, the queen's daughter came to the well at the world's end. She lowered her bottle, but like the king's daughter, found that it would not reach the water in the well. Then she heard the three old men speaking: "Wash us, wash us, fair maid, and dry us with your linen apron."

And the proud daughter replied, "You

224

nasty, filthy creatures, do you think a queen's daughter can be bothered to wash you, and dry your dirty faces with my fine clean clothes?"

So the old men refused to dip the girl's bottle into the well. Instead, they turned to her and began to predict her future: "If she was ugly before, she will be ten times uglier," said the first.

"Each time she speaks, a frog and a toad will jump from her mouth," predicted the second.

"When she combs her hair, lice and fleas will appear," said the third.

With these curses ringing in her ears, the unhappy girl returned home. Her mother was distraught when she saw her daughter, for she was indeed uglier than before, and frogs, toads, fleas, and lice, jumped from her. In the end, she left the king's court, and married a poor cobbler. The king's fair and good-natured daughter married a handsome prince, and was happy – and good-natured – for the rest of her long life.

225

 18 AUGUST

# MY GRANDMOTHER SENT ME

My grandmother sent me a new-fashioned three cornered cambric country cut handkerchief. Not an old-fashioned three cornered cambric country cut handkerchief, but a new-fashioned three cornered cambric country cut handkerchief.

19 AUGUST

# ROBERT ROWLEY

Robert Rowley rolled a round roll round,
A round roll Robert Rowley rolled round;
Where rolled the round roll Robert Rowley
   rolled round?

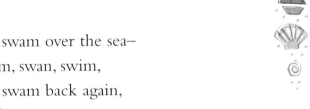

## 20 AUGUST

# SWAN SWAM OVER THE SEA

Swan swam over the sea–
Swim, swan, swim,
Swan swam back again,
Well swum swan.

## 21 AUGUST

# HEY, DOROLOT, DOROLOT!

Hey, dorolot, dorolot!
Hey, dorolay, dorolay!
Hey, my bonny boat, bonny boat,
Hey, drag away, drag away!

# THERE WAS A MAN AND HIS NAME WAS DOB

There was a man, and his name was Dob,
And he had a wife, and her name was Mob,
And he had a dog, and he called it Cob,
And she had a cat, called Chitterabob.
  Cob, says Dob,
  Chitterabob, says Mob,
  Cob was Dob's dog,
  Chitterabob Mob's cat.

# DIBBITY, DIBBITY, DIBBITY, DOE

Dibbity, dibbity, dibbity, doe,
Give me a pancake
  And I'll go.
Dibbity, dibbity, dibbity, ditter,
Please to give me
  A bit of a fritter.

# A THORN

I went to the wood and got it;
I sat me down and looked at it;
The more I looked at it the less I liked it;
And I brought it home because I couldn't help it.

24 AUGUST

# TEETH

Thirty white horses upon a red hill,
Now they tramp, now they champ,
now they stand still.

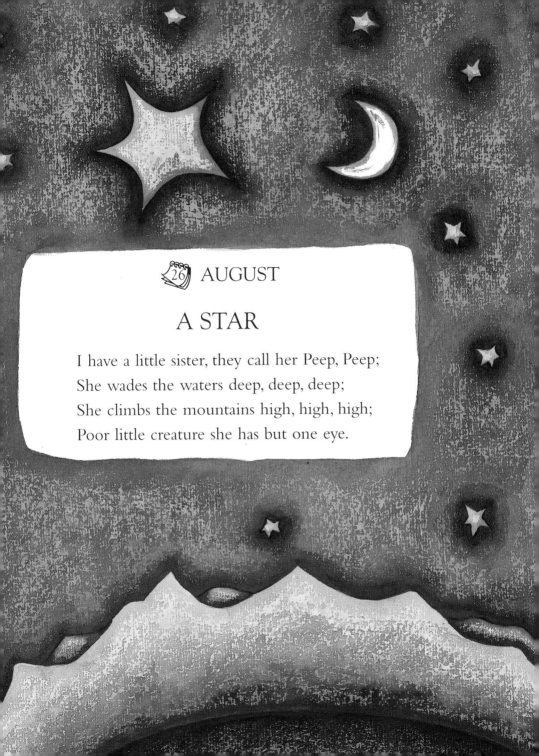

# 26 AUGUST

## A STAR

I have a little sister, they call her Peep, Peep;
She wades the waters deep, deep, deep;
She climbs the mountains high, high, high;
Poor little creature she has but one eye.

 AUGUST

If the moon came from heaven,
   Talking all the way,
What could she have to tell us,
   And what could she say?

'I've seen a hundred pretty things,
   And seen a hundred gay;
But only think: I peep by night
   And do not peep by day!'

 AUGUST

Is the moon tired? she looks so pale
   Within her misty veil:
She scales the sky from east to west,
   And takes no rest.

 AUGUST

Before the coming of the night
   The moon shows papery white;
Before the dawning of the day
   She fades away.

 AUGUST

How many seconds in a minute?
Sixty, and no more in it.

 AUGUST

Fly away, fly away over the sea,
   Sun-loving swallow, for summer is done;
Come again, come again, come back to me,
   Bringing the summer and bringing the sun.

 SEPTEMBER

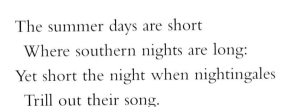

The summer nights are short
   Where northern days are long:
For hours and hours lark after lark
   Trills out his song.

The summer days are short
   Where southern nights are long:
Yet short the night when nightingales
   Trill out their song.

# TOMMY TROT

Tommy Trot, a man of law,
Sold his bed and lay upon straw:
Sold the straw and slept on grass,
To buy his wife a looking-glass.

# 3 SEPTEMBER

## TUMBLING

In jumping and tumbling
We spend the whole day,
Till night by arriving
Has finished our play.

What then? One and all,
There's no more to be said,
As we tumbled all day,
So we tumble to bed.

SEPTEMBER

# HUSH, LITTLE BABY

Hush, little baby, don't say a word,
Papa's going to buy you a mocking bird.

If the mocking bird won't sing,
Papa's going to buy you a diamond ring.

If the diamond ring turn to brass,
Papa's going to buy you a looking-glass.

If the looking-glass gets broke,
Papa's going to buy you a billy-goat.

If that billy-goat runs away,
Papa's going to buy you another today.

ANONYMOUS
AMERICAN

5 SEPTEMBER

# THE MOUSE'S LULLABY

Oh, rock-a-by, baby mouse, rock-a-by, so!
When baby's asleep to the baker's I'll go,
And while he's not looking I'll pop from a hole,
And bring to my baby a fresh penny roll.

PALMER COX

## 6 SEPTEMBER

# A CRADLE SONG

Golden slumbers kiss your eyes,
Smiles awake you when you rise.
Sleep, pretty wantons, do not cry,
And I will sing a lullaby:
Rock them, rock them, lullaby.

Care is heavy, therefore sleep you;
You are care, and care must keep you.
Sleep, pretty wantons, do not cry,
And I will sing a lullaby:
Rock them, rock them, lullaby.

THOMAS DEKKER

# A CHILD'S EVENING PRAYER

Ere on my bed my limbs I lay,
God grant me grace my prayers to say:
O God, preserve my mother dear
In strength and health for many a year;
And, O! preserve my father too,
And may I pay him reverence due;
And may I my best thoughts employ
To be my parents' hope and joy;
And O! preserve my brothers both
From evil doings and from sloth,
And may we always love each other
Our friends, our father, and our mother:
And still, O Lord, to me impart
An innocent and grateful heart,
That after my great sleep I may
Awake to thy eternal day! Amen.

SAMUEL TAYLOR COLERIDGE

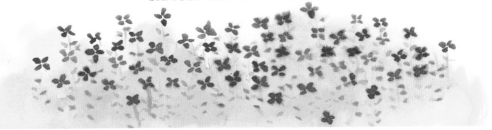

# SONG OF THE SKY LOOM

O our Mother the Earth, O our Father the Sky,
Your children are we, and with tired backs
We bring you the gifts that you love.
Then weave for us a garment of brightness;
May the warp be the white light of morning,
May the weft be the red light of evening,
May the fringes be the falling rain,
May the border be the standing rainbow.
Thus weave for us a garment of brightness,
That we may walk fittingly where birds sing,
That we way walk fittingly where grass is green,
O our Mother the Earth, O our Father the sky.

ANONYMOUS
NATIVE AMERICAN, TEWA

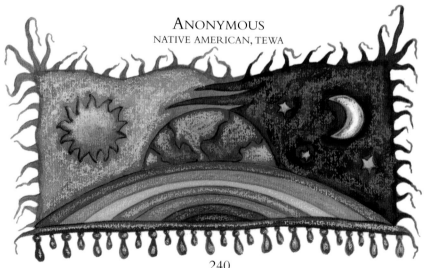

240

# PUTTING THE WORLD TO BED

The little snow people are hurrying down
  From their home in the clouds overhead;
They are working as hard as ever they can,
  Putting the world to bed.

Every tree in a soft fleecy nightgown they clothe;
  Each part has its night-cap of white.
And o'er the cold ground a thick cover they spread
  Before they say good-night.

And so they come eagerly sliding down,
  With a swift and silent tread,
Always as busy as busy can be,
  Putting the world to bed.

ESTHER W. BUXTON

241

# THE SPRIGHTLY TAILOR

Long ago, in a castle called Sandell, lived a laird called the great MacDonald. MacDonald liked his comfort, and favoured garments called trews, which were a combination of vest and trousers in one piece. One day the laird needed some new trews, and called for the local tailor.

When the tailor arrived the great MacDonald told him what he wanted. "I'll pay you extra," promised the laird, "if you will make the trews in the church by night." For MacDonald had heard that the church was haunted by a fearful monster, and he

wanted to see how the tailor fared when faced with this beast.

The tailor had also heard stories about the monster. But he was a sprightly fellow who liked a challenge – especially if it was going to lead to some extra money. So that very night he walked up the glen, through the churchyard gate, and into

242

the dark church. Finding a tombstone where he could sit, he got to work on the trews, and very soon the garment was taking shape.

After a while, the tailor felt the floor of the church begin to shake beneath him. A hole seemed to open up in the stone floor and a large and gruesome head appeared. "Do you see this great head of mine?" a voice boomed.

"I see that, but I'll sew these," replied the tailor, holding up the trews.

The head paused as the tailor was speaking, then began to rise again, revealing a thick, muscular neck. "Do you see this great neck of mine?" the monster asked.

"I see that, but I'll sew these," replied the tailor.

Next the creature's shoulders and trunk came into view. "Do you see this great chest of mine?"

"I see that, but I'll sew these," said the tailor. And he carried on sewing, although, to tell the truth, some of the stitches were a little less neat than normal.

Now the beast was rising quickly, and the tailor could make

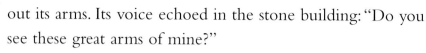

out its arms. Its voice echoed in the stone building: "Do you see these great arms of mine?"

"I see those, but I'll sew these," replied the tailor. He gritted his teeth and carried on with his work as before, for he wanted to finish by daybreak and claim his payment from the great MacDonald.

The tailor's needle was flying now, as the monster gave a great grunt and lifted his first leg out of the ground. "Do you see this great leg of mine?" he said, his voice getting even louder.

"I see that, but I'll sew these," replied the tailor, making his final stitches a little longer, so that he could finish his work before the monster could climb out of his hole.

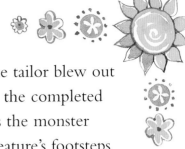

As the creature began to raise its other leg, the tailor blew out his candle, gathered up his things, and bundled the completed trews under one arm. He made for the door as the monster was emerging, and the tailor could hear the creature's footsteps echoing on the stone floor as he ran out into the open air.

Now the tailor could see the glen stretching in front of him, and he ran for his life, faster than he had ever ran before, for all that he was a nimble man. The monster roared at him to stop, but the tailor hurried on, his feet hardly touching the ground, and finally the great MacDonald's castle loomed up ahead of him and the tailor knew he had a chance to reach its gates.

Quickly the gates opened, and quickly they closed behind the tailor – and not a moment too soon, for as the great wooden gates slammed shut, the monster crashed to a halt and struck a resounding blow on the wall to show how frustrated he was at missing his goal when he had got so near.

To this day, the monster's handprint can be seen on the wall of the castle at Sandell. MacDonald paid the sprightly tailor for his work, and gave him a handsome bonus for braving the haunted church. The laird liked his smart new trews, and never realised that some of the stitches were longer and less neat than the others.

## 11 SEPTEMBER

# NIGHT SOUNDS

Midnight's bell goes ting, ting, ting, ting, ting,
Then dogs do howl, and not a bird does sing
But the nightingale, and she cries twit, twit, twit;
Owls then on every bough do sit;
Ravens croak on chimneys' tops;
The cricket in the chamber hops;
The nibbling mouse is not asleep,
But he goes peep, peep, peep, peep, peep;
  And the cats cry mew, mew, mew,
  And still the cats cry mew, mew, mew.

THOMAS MIDDLETON

## SEPTEMBER

# SWEET AND LOW

Sweet and low, sweet and low,
    Wind of the western sea,
Low, low, breathe and blow,
    Wind of the western sea!
Over the rolling waters go,
Come from the dying moon, and blow,
    Blow him again to me;
While my little one, while my pretty one, sleeps.

Sleep and rest, sleep and rest,
    Father will come to thee soon;
Rest, rest, on mother's breast,
    Father will come to thee soon;
Father will come to his babe in the nest,
Silver sails all out of the west
    Under the silver moon:
Sleep, my little one, sleep, my pretty one, sleep.

ALFRED, LORD TENNYSON

# DREAMS

Beyond, beyond the mountain line,
  The grey-stone and the boulder,
Beyond the growth of dark green pine,
  That crowns its western shoulder,
There lies that fairy land of mine,
  Unseen of a beholder.

Its fruits are all like rubies rare,
  Its streams are clear as glasses:
There golden castles hang in air,
  And purple grapes in masses,
And noble knights and ladies fair
  Come riding down the passes.

Ah me! they say if I could stand
  Upon those mountain ledges,
I should but see on either hand
  Plain fields and dusty hedges:
And yet I know my fairy land
  Lies somewhere o'er their hedges.

CECIL FRANCES ALEXANDER

248

 SEPTEMBER

# DREAMS

Here we are all, by day; by night we are hurled
By dreams, each one into a several world.

ROBERT HERRICK

# I HAD A LITTLE NUT TREE

I had a little nut tree, nothing would it bear,
But a silver nutmeg, and a golden pear;
The King of Spain's daughter came to visit me,
And all for the sake of my little nut tree.
I skipped over water, I danced over sea,
And all the birds of the air couldn't catch me.

 SEPTEMBER

# HOW MANY MILES TO BABYLON?

How many miles to Babylon?–
Threescore and ten.
Can I get there by candlelight?–
Aye, and back again!

# LADY MOON

Lady Moon, Lady Moon, where are you roving?
    Over the sea.
Lady Moon, Lady Moon, whom are you loving?
    All that love me.

Are you not tired with rolling, and never
    Resting to sleep?
Why look so pale, and so sad, as for ever
    Wishing to weep?

Ask me not this, little child, if you love me;
    You are too bold;
I must obey my dear Father above me,
    And do as I'm told.

Lady Moon, Lady Moon, where are you roving?
    Over the sea.
Lady Moon, Lady Moon, whom are you loving?
    All that love me.

RICHARD MONCKTON MILNES, LORD HOUGHTON

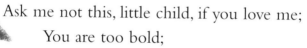

# THE MOON

The moon has a face like the clock in the hall;
She shines on thieves on the garden wall,
On streets and fields and harbour quays,
And birdies asleep in the forks of the trees.

The squalling cat and the squeaking mouse,
The howling dog by the door of the house,
The bat that lies in bed at noon,
All love to be out by the light of the moon.

But all of the things that belong to the day
Cuddle to sleep to be out of her way;
And flowers and children close their eyes
Till up in the morning the sun shall arise.

ROBERT LOUIS STEVENSON

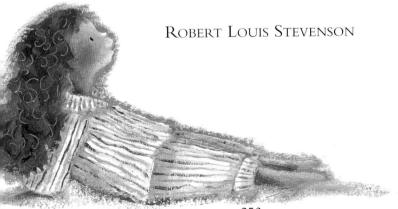

# MR FROGGIE WENT A-COURTIN'

Mr Froggie went a-courtin' an' he did ride;
Sword and pistol by his side.

He went to Missus Mousie's hall,
Gave a loud knock and gave a loud call.

"Pray, Missus Mousie, air you within?"
"Yes, kind sir, I set an' spin."

He tuk Miss Mousie on his knee,
An' sez, "Miss Mousie, will ya marry me?"

Miss Mousie blushed an' hung her head,
"You'll have t'ask Uncle Rat," she said.

"Not without Uncle Rat's consent
Would I marry the Pres-i-dent."

Uncle Rat jumped up an' shuck his fat side,
To think his niece would be Bill Frog's bride.

Nex' day Uncle Rat went to town,
To git his niece a weddin' gown.

Whar shall the weddin' supper be?
'Way down yander in a holler tree.

First come in was a Bumble-bee,
Who danced a jig with Captain Flea.

Next come in was a Butterfly,
Sellin' butter very high.

An' when they all set down to sup,
A big gray goose come an' gobbled 'em all up.

An' this is the end of one, two, three,
The Rat an' the Mouse an' the little Froggie.

ANONYMOUS
AMERICAN

# THE DUEL

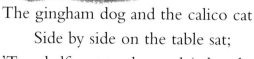

The gingham dog and the calico cat
    Side by side on the table sat;
'Twas half-past twelve, and (what do you think!)
Nor one nor t'other had slept a wink!
    The old Dutch clock and the Chinese plate
    Appeared to know as sure as fate
There was going to be a terrible spat.
    *(I wasn't there; I simply state*
    *What was told to me by the Chinese plate!)*

The gingham dog went "Bow-wow-wow!
And the calico cat replied "mee-ow!"
The air was littered, an hour or so,
With bits of gingham and calico,
    While the old Dutch clock in the chimney-place
    Up with its hands before its face,
For it always dreaded a family row!
    *(Now mind: I'm only telling you*
    *What the old Dutch clock declares is true!)*

Mee-ow

Bow-wow-wow

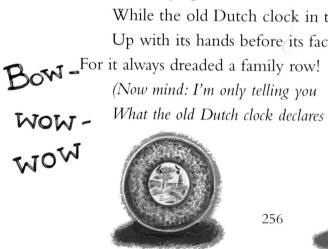

The Chinese plate looked very blue,
And wailed, "Oh, dear! what shall we do?"
But the gingham dog and the calico cat
Wallowed this way and tumbled that,
    Employing every tooth and claw
    In the awfullest way you ever saw—
And, oh! how the gingham and calico flew!
    *(Don't fancy I exaggerate!*
    *I got my news from the Chinese plate!)*

Next morning, where the two had sat,
They found no trace of dog or cat;
And some folks think unto this day
That burglars stole that pair away!
    But the truth about the cat and pup
    Is this: they ate each other up!
Now what do you really think of that!
    *(The old Dutch clock it told me so,*
    *And that is how I came to know.)*

EUGENE FIELD

# ELDORADO

Gaily bedight
A gallant knight,
In sunshine and in shadow,
Had journeyed long,
Singing a song,
In search of Eldorado.

But he grew old–
This knight so bold–
And o'er his heart a shadow
Fell as he found
No spot of ground
That looked like Eldorado.

And, as his strength
Failed him at length,
He met a pilgrim shadow:
"Shadow," said he,
"Where can it be,
This land of Eldorado?"

"Over the mountains
Of the Moon,
Down the valley of the Shadow,
Ride, boldly ride,"
The shade replied,
"If you seek for Eldorado."

EDGAR ALLAN POE

# THE WAR SONG OF DINAS VAWR

The mountain sheep are sweeter,
But the valley sheep are fatter;
We therefore deemed it meeter
To carry off the latter.
We made an expedition;
We met a host and quelled it;
We forced a strong position,
And killed the men who held it.

On Dyfed's richest valley,
Where herds of kine were browsing,
We made a mighty sally,
To furnish our carousing.
Fierce warriors rushed to meet us;
We met them and o'erthrew them:
They struggled hard to beat us;
But we conquered them, and slew them.

As we drove our prize at leisure,
The king marched forth to catch us;
His rage surpassed all measure,
But his people could not match us.
He fled to his hall pillars;

And, ere our force we led off,
Some sacked his house and cellars,
While others cut his head off.

We there, in strife bewildering,
Spilt blood enough to swim in:
We orphaned many children,
And widowed many women.
The eagles and the ravens
We glutted with our foemen:
The heroes and the cravens,
The spearmen and the bowmen.

We brought away from battle,
And much their land bemoaned them,
Two thousand head of cattle,
And the head of him who owned them:
Edynfed, King of Dyfed,
His head was borne before us;
His wine and beasts supplied our feasts,
And his overthrow, our chorus.

THOMAS LOVE PEACOCK

261

 SEPTEMBER

# THE CRY OF VENGEANCE

Long ago in the ancient town of Bala lived a wicked prince called Tegid Foel. All his people feared him, for if anyone got in his way, or disagreed with him, the prince had them killed.

Some men plotted to dethrone the prince, but none of them succeeded, for Tegid Foel surrounded himself with guards and henchmen who were almost as ruthless as himself. One day, the prince heard a small voice, whispering in his ear, "Vengeance will come, vengeance will come!" Tegid took no

notice of the voice, even though he heard it again, and soon he heard it every day. And the prince's rule carried on for many years of cruelty, until his three sons were grown up and his first son was married.

Tegid Foel's castle was usually a quiet, sombre place, but one day there was noise of rejoicing there. The wife of Tegid's first son had given birth to her first child, a grandson for the prince, and a great feast was ordered. Everyone in the kingdom was invited – and woe betide anyone who did not attend.

One of those who did not want to come was a young, peace-loving harper from the hills near Bala. He was known as the best musician for miles around, and Tegid wanted him to play at his feast. The harper knew that there would be trouble if he did not go, so he took his harp and strode to the castle.

When the harper arrived, the banquet was already beginning, so he took his place as quickly as he could and began to tune his instrument. When the prince saw him, he roared "Waste no time! Play, harper!" in a voice that sent a chill through all who heard. So the harper sang and played, to the delight of everyone in the hall. It seemed as if his music had brought some tranquillity and beauty to the place, where the atmosphere was usually brooding and evil.

At around midnight, there was an interval, and the harper strolled outside in the courtyard to relax for a while. As he did so, a voice whispered in his ear, "Vengeance has come, vengeance has come." Then he saw a small bird that seemed to be beckoning to him with its beak. The creature seemed to be telling him to leave the castle.

At first, the harper was doubtful, and he wondered what would become of him if he left the banquet now. But he had always listened to the sounds of nature, so he decided to obey the call, slipping through the castle gates and making for the hills. When he had walked for a while, the harper paused. He realized in horror that he had left his harp behind him in the hall. At once he was in turmoil. His harp was his livelihood. But the guards had probably already noticed that he had gone. If he returned – either to play or to take the harp – he risked losing his head. So he decided to continue on his way.

Far the harper climbed into the hills, leaving the sounds of revelling behind him, until he began to tire and could walk no more. He felt that he was far enough away to be out of reach of the castle guards, who were anyway too intent on revelling to chase him tonight. So he lay down and fell asleep.

At dawn, the harper awoke and stretched and rubbed his eyes. As he looked down to the valley he saw an astounding sight. The town and castle of Bala were no more. In their place was a gigantic lake. The only sign of the previous night's feast was his harp, floating unharmed. As the ripples of the water brought the instrument back to him, the harper sighed with relief that he had listened to the quiet, sweet voice of the bird instead of the harsh, ugly voice of the prince's command.

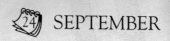 SEPTEMBER

# THERE'S A HOLE IN THE MIDDLE OF THE SEA

There's a hole, there's a hole,
   there's a hole in the middle of the sea.

There's a log in the hole in the middle of the sea.

There's a hole, there's a hole,
   there's a hole in the middle of the sea.

There's a bump on the log in the
   hole in the middle of the sea.

There's a hole, there's a hole,
   there's a hole in the middle of the sea.

There's a frog on the bump on the log
   in the hole in the middle of the sea.

There's a hole, there's a hole,
   there's a hole in the middle of the sea.

There's a fly on the frog on the bump
  on the log in the hole in the middle of the sea.

There's a hole, there's a hole,
  there's a hole in the middle of the sea.

There's a wing on the fly on the frog on the
  bump on the log in the hole in the middle of the sea.

There's a hole, there's a hole,
  there's a hole in the middle of the sea.

There's a flea on the wing on the fly
  on the frog on the bump on the log in the
  hole in the middle of the sea.

There's a hole, there's a hole,
  there's a hole in the middle of the sea.

ANONYMOUS
AMERICAN

# THERE WAS AN OLD WOMAN
# WHO LIVED IN A SHOE

There was an old woman who lived in a shoe,
She had so many children she didn't know
  what to do;
She gave them some broth without any bread;
And scolded them soundly and put them to bed.

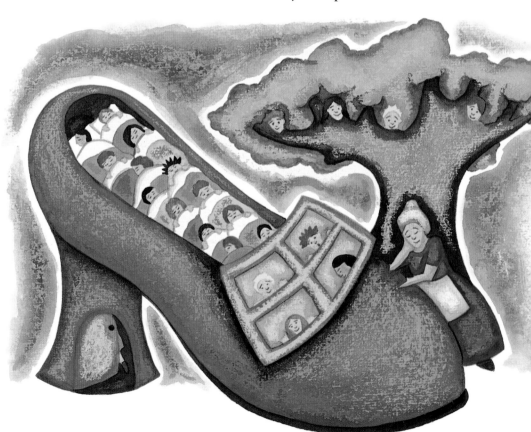

# THERE WAS AN OLD WOMAN, AND WHAT DO YOU THINK?

There was an old woman, and what do you think?
She lived upon nothing but victuals and drink:
Victuals and drink were the chief of her diet;
This tiresome old woman could never be quiet.

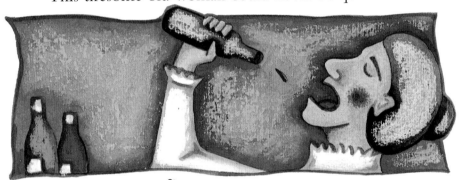

 SEPTEMBER

# THERE WAS AN OLD WOMAN CALLED NOTHING-AT-ALL

There was an old woman called Nothing-at-all,
Who rejoiced in a dwelling exceedingly small;
A man stretched his mouth to its utmost extent,
And down at one gulp house and old woman went.

# THERE WAS AN OLD WOMAN LIVED UNDER A HILL

There was old woman
Lived under a hill,
And if she's not gone
She lives there still.

 SEPTEMBER

# THERE WAS AN OLD WOMAN HAD THREE SONS

There was an old woman had three sons,
Jerry, and James, and John:
Jerry was hung, James was drowned,
John was lost and never was found,
And there was an end of the three sons,
Jerry, and James, and John!

## 30 SEPTEMBER

# THERE WAS AN OLD WOMAN
# WENT UP IN A BASKET

There was an old woman went up in a basket,
Seventy times as high as the moon;
What she did there I could not but ask it,
For in her hand she carried a broom.
"Old woman, old woman, old woman," said I,
"Whither oh whither oh whither so high?"
"To sweep the cobwebs from the sky,
And I shall be back again by and by."

# OCTOBER

## OLD BETTY BLUE

Old Betty Blue
  Lost a holiday shoe,
What can old Betty do?
  Give her another
  To match the other,
And then she may swagger in two.

# OLD MOTHER GOOSE

Old Mother Goose, when
She wanted to wander,
Would ride through the air
On a very fine gander.

# ONE MISTY MOISTY MORNING

One misty moisty morning,
When cloudy was the weather,
There I met an old man
Clothed all in leather;

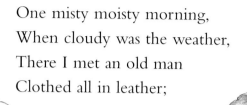

Clothed all in leather,
With cap under his chin–
How do you do, and how do you do,
And how do you do again!

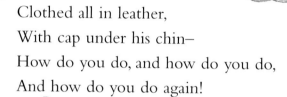

 OCTOBER

# THERE WAS A CROOKED MAN

There was a crooked man, and he went a
  crooked mile,
He found a crooked sixpence against a
  crooked stile;
He bought a crooked cat, which caught a
  crooked mouse,
And they all lived together in a little crooked house.

# AS I WALKED BY MYSELF

As I walked by myself,
And talked to myself,
  Myself said unto me,
Look to thyself,
Take care of thyself,
  For nobody cares for thee.

I answered myself,
And said to myself,
  In the self-same repartee,
Look to thyself,
Or not look to thyself,
  The self-same thing will be.

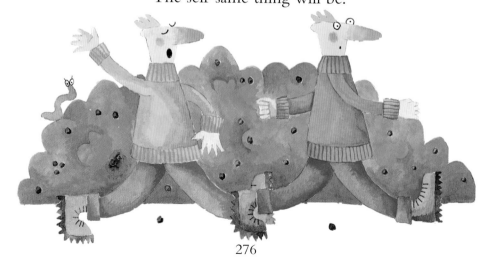

 OCTOBER

# CROSS PATCH

Cross patch,
 Draw the latch,
Sit by the fire and spin;
 Take a cup,
 And drink it up,
Then call your neighbours in.

 OCTOBER

# IT'S RAINING, IT'S POURING

It's raining, it's pouring,
The old man is snoring;
He went to bed and bumped his head
And couldn't get up in the morning.

 OCTOBER

# THE MAIDEN FROM THE LAKE

There was once a shepherd who lived in Myddvai, by the mountains of Caermarthen. A great lake was near his pastures, and one day he was watching his sheep near its shores when he saw three beautiful maidens rise from the waters. The young women came to the shore, shook the water from their hair, and walked around among the sheep.

The shepherd was overcome by the beauty of the maiden who came nearest to him, and he offered her some bread from his pack. The girl took the bread, tried a little, and said to the shepherd, "Your bread's too hard. You won't catch me." Then she ran back to the lake with the others.

The shepherd wondered whether he would see the maidens again, but just in case, on the next day, he brought some bread that was not so well baked. To his delight, the maidens appeared again, and he offered the softer bread. But this time the girl said, "Your bread's not baked. You won't catch me." Once more, she returned to the water.

On the third day, the shepherd waited for the young woman. When she came, he offered her some bread that had been

floating on the water. This she liked, and the couple talked for a long while. Finally, the maiden agreed to marry the shepherd, but gave this warning: she would be a good wife to him, as good as any ordinary Welsh woman, unless he struck her three times without reason. The shepherd vowed that he would never do this, and the couple were soon married.

The shepherd and his bride were happy, and in time had three fine sons. It happened that they were going to christen one of the children when the wife said that it was too far to walk to church.

"Then go and get the horses," said the shepherd, "and we will ride all the way."

"While I get the horses, will you fetch my gloves from the house?" asked his wife.

But when the shepherd returned with the gloves he found that she had not fetched the horses, and he tapped her gently on the shoulder to remind her.

"That's one strike," said his wife.

A little while later, the pair were at a friend's wedding. The shepherd found his wife crying and again he tapped her on the shoulder as he asked her what was wrong.

"Trouble is coming for you," she replied. "That is the second time you have struck me without reason. Take care to avoid the third time."

From then on, the shepherd was careful not so much as to tap his wife, until one day the couple were at a funeral. All of a sudden, the wife began to laugh loudly. The shepherd was amazed. He could not understand why anyone should laugh at such a sad time, so, touching her rather roughly, he said, "Wife, why are you laughing when all around you are sad?"

"I am laughing because people who die leave their troubles behind them. But your troubles have just begun. You have struck me for a third time. Now I must make an end to our marriage and bid you farewell."

The shepherd knew that the time had come for his wife to leave him, and he was sad to the bottom of his heart. But he was still more surprised when he heard his wife calling all the cattle around her, bidding them follow her to her home

beneath the waters of the lake. He saw all his cattle, even a black calf that had recently been slaughtered and a team of oxen that were ploughing a field, get up and follow her away. The oxen even took their plough with them, cutting a deep furrow all the way to the shore.

The mark left by the plough can still be seen running across the pastures by the lake. But the lady has only been seen once more. When her sons had grown up, she returned to visit them. She gave them miraculous gifts of healing. And ever since, the Doctors of Myddvai have been famous throughout the land of Wales.

281

# WHEN I WAS A BACHELOR

When I was a bachelor I lived by myself,
And all the meat I got I put upon a shelf;
The rats and the mice did lead me such a life
That I went to London to get myself a wife.

The streets were so broad and the lanes were
   so narrow,
I could not get my wife home without a
   wheelbarrow;
The wheelbarrow broke, my wife got a fall,
Down tumbled wheelbarrow, little wife, and all.

# JACK SPRAT

Jack Sprat could eat no fat,
   His wife could eat no lean,
And so between the two of them
   They licked the platter clean.

# OLD JOE BROWN

Old Joe Brown, he had a wife,
  She was all of eight feet tall.
She slept with her head in the kitchen,
  And her feet stuck out in the hall.

# JEREMIAH

Jeremiah
Jumped in the fire.
Fire was so hot
He jumped in the pot.
Pot was so little
He jumped in the kettle.
Kettle was so black
He jumped in the crack.
Crack was so high
He jumped in the sky.
Sky was so blue
He jumped in a canoe.
Canoe was so deep
He jumped in the creek.
Creek was so shallow
He jumped in the tallow.
Tallow was so soft
He jumped in the loft.
Loft was so rotten
He jumped in the cotton.
Cotton was so white
He jumped all night.

 OCTOBER

# OLD JOHN MUDDLECOMBE

Old John Muddlecombe lost his cap,
He couldn't find it anywhere, the poor old chap.
He walked down the High Street, and everybody said,
"Silly John Muddlecombe, you've got it on your head!"

# POOR OLD ROBINSON CRUSOE

Poor old Robinson Crusoe!
Poor old Robinson Crusoe!
They made him a coat
Of an old nanny goat,
I wonder how they could do so!
With a ring a ting tang,
And a ring a ting tang,
Poor old Robinson Crusoe!

 OCTOBER

# RUB-A-DUB DUB

Rub-a-dub dub,
Three men in a tub,
And who do you think they be?
The butcher, the baker,
The candle-stick maker,
And they all jumped out of a rotten potato.

# DOCTOR FOSTER WENT TO GLOUCESTER

Doctor Foster went to Gloucester,
  In a shower of rain;
He stepped in a puddle, right up to his
middle, And never went there again.

 ## OCTOBER

There was an old person of Harrow,
Who bought a mahogany barrow,
For he said to his wife, "You're the joy of my life!
And I'll wheel you all day in this barrow!"

 ## OCTOBER

Hush-a-bye baby, they've gone to milk,
Lady and milkmaid all in silk,
Lady goes softly, maid goes slow,
Round again, round again, round they go!

 ## OCTOBER

There was an old man, who when little
Fell casually into a kettle;
But, growing too stout, he could never get out,
So he passed all his life in that kettle.

 ## OCTOBER

Hannah Bantry in the pantry,
Eating a mutton bone,
How she gnawed it, how she clawed it,
When she thought she was alone!

##  OCTOBER

There was a young lady whose chin,
Resembled the point of a pin;
So she had it made sharp, and purchased a harp,
And played several tunes with her chin.

##  OCTOBER

Oh, dear, what can the matter be?
Two old ladies stuck up an apple-tree!
One came down,
But the other stayed till Saturday!

##  OCTOBER

Little cock-robin peeped out of his cabin,
To see the cold winter come in.
Tit for tat, what matter that,
He'll hide his head under his wing!

## 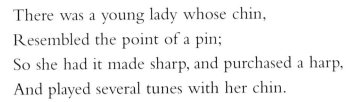 OCTOBER

There was an old man who said, "Well!
Will *nobody* answer this bell?
I have pulled day and night, till my hair has grown white,
But nobody answers this bell!"

# PETER, PETER, PUMPKIN EATER

Peter, Peter, pumpkin eater,
Had a wife and couldn't keep her;
He put her in a pumpkin shell
And there he kept her very well.

Peter, Peter, pumpkin eater,
Had another and didn't love her;
Peter learned to read and spell,
And then he loved her very well.

 OCTOBER

# SIMPLE SIMON

Simple Simon met a pieman
  Going to the fair;
Said Simple Simon to the pieman,
  "Let me taste your ware."

Said the pieman to Simple Simon,
  "Show me first your penny;"
Said Simple Simon to the pieman,
  "Indeed I have not any."

 OCTOBER

# UNCLE JOHN IS VERY SICK

Uncle John is very sick, what shall we send him?
A piece of pie, a piece of cake, a piece of apple dumpling.
What shall we send it in? In a piece of paper.
Paper is not fine enough; in a golden saucer.
Who shall we send it by? By the governor's daughter.
Take her by the lily-white hand, and lead her over the water.

 OCTOBER

# AT THE SIEGE OF BELLE-ISLE

At the siege of Belle-isle
I was there all the while.

# AUTUMN FIRES

In the other gardens
   And all up the vale,
From the autumn bonfires
   See the smoke trail!

Pleasant summer over
   And all the summer flowers,
The red fire blazes,
   The grey smoke towers.

Sing a song of seasons!
   Something bright in all!
Flowers in the summer,
   Fires in the fall!

ROBERT LOUIS STEVENSON

# THE ENCHANTMENT OF EARL GERALD

Earl Gerald was one of the bravest leaders in Ireland long ago. He lived in a castle at Mullaghmast with his lady and his knights, and whenever Ireland was attacked, Earl Gerald was among the first to join the fight to defend his homeland.

As well as being a great fighter, Gerald was also a magician who could change himself into any shape or form that he wanted. His wife was fascinated by this, but had never seen Gerald change his shape, although she had often asked him to show her how he could transform himself into the shape of some strange beast. Gerald always put her off with some excuse, until one day her pleading got too much for him.

"Very well," said Earl Gerald. "I will do what you ask. But you must promise not to show any fear when I change my shape. If you are frightened, I will not be able to change myself back again for hundreds of years."

She protested that the wife of such a noble warrior, who had seen him ride into battle against fearsome enemies, would not be frightened by such a small thing, so Gerald agreed to change his shape.

They were sitting quietly in the great chamber of the castle when suddenly Gerald vanished and a beautiful goldfinch was flying around the room. His wife was shocked by the sudden change, but did her best to stay calm and keep her side of the bargain. All went well, and she watched the little bird fly out into the garden, return, and perch in her lap. Gerald's wife was delighted with the bird, and smiled merrily, when suddenly and without warning, a great hawk swooped through the open windows, diving towards the finch. The lady screamed, even though the hawk missed Gerald and crashed into the table top, where its sharp beak stuck into the wood.

The damage was done. Gerald's wife had shown her fear. As she looked down to where the goldfinch had perched, she

realised that the tiny bird had vanished. She never saw either the goldfinch or Earl Gerald again.

Many hundreds of years have passed by since Earl Gerald disappeared, and his poor wife is long dead. But occasionally, Gerald may be seen. Once in seven years, he mounts his steed and is seen riding around the Curragh of Kildare. Those few who have glimpsed him say that his horse has shoes made of silver, and the story goes that when these shoes are finally worn away, Gerald will return, fight a great battle, and rule as King of Ireland for forty years.

Meanwhile, in a great cavern beneath the old castle of Mullaghmast, Gerald and his knights sleep their long sleep. They are dressed in full armour and sit around a long table with the Earl at the head. Their horses, saddled and bridled, stand ready. When the right moment comes, a young lad with six fingers on each hand will blow a trumpet to awaken them.

Once, almost one hundred years ago, Earl Gerald was on one of his seven-yearly rides and an old horse-dealer was passing the cavern where Gerald's knights were still sleeping. There were lights in the cavern, and the horse-dealer went in to have a look. He was amazed to see the knights in their armour, all slumped on the table fast asleep, and the fine horses waiting there. He was looking at their steeds, and thinking whether he might lead one of the beasts away to market, when he dropped

the bridle he was holding. The clattering of the falling bridle echoed in the cavern and one of the knights stirred in his slumber.

"Has the time come?" groaned the knight, his voice husky with sleep. The horse-dealer was struck dumb for a moment, as the knight's voice echoed in the cave. Finally he replied.

"No, the time has not come yet. But it soon will."

The knight slumped back on to the table, his helmet giving a heavy clank on the board. The horse-dealer ran away home with all the speed he could manage. And Earl Gerald's knights slept on.

# EVENING

*(In words of one syllable)*

The day is past, the sun is set,
  And the white stars are in the sky;
While the long grass with dew is wet,
  And through the air the bats now fly.

The lambs have now lain down to sleep,
  The birds have long since sought their nests;
The air is still, and dark, and deep
  On the hill side the old wood rests.

Yet of the dark I have no fear,
  But feel as safe as when 'tis light;
For I know God is with me there,
  And He will guard me through the night.

For God is by me when I pray,
  And when I close mine eyes in sleep,
I know that He will with me stay,
  And will all night watch by me keep.

For He who rules the stars and sea,
　Who makes the grass and trees to grow,
Will look on a poor child like me,
　When on my knees I to Him bow.

He holds all things in His right hand,
　The rich, the poor, the great, the small;
When we sleep, or sit, or stand,
　Is with us, for He loves us all.

THOMAS MILLER

 NOVEMBER

# THE SONG OF THE STARS

We are the stars which sing,
We sing with our light.
We are the birds of fire
We fly over the sky,
Our light is a voice.
We make a road for spirits,
For the spirits to pass over.

Among us are three hunters
Who chase a bear;
There never was a time
When they were not hunting.
We look down on the mountains.
This is the song of the stars.

ANONYMOUS
NATIVE AMERICAN, PASSAMAQUODDY

# MINNIE AND WINNIE

Minnie and Winnie
  Slept in a shell.
Sleep, little ladies!
  And they slept well.

Pink was the shell within,
  Silver without;
Sounds of the great sea
  Wandered about.

Sleep, little ladies,
  Wake not soon!
Echo on echo
  Dies to the moon.

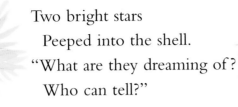

Two bright stars
 Peeped into the shell.
"What are they dreaming of?
 Who can tell?"

Started a green linnet
 Out of the croft;
Wake, little ladies,
 The sun is aloft!

A<small>LFRED</small>, L<small>ORD</small> T<small>ENNYSON</small>

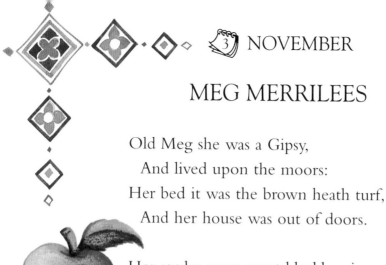

# MEG MERRILEES

Old Meg she was a Gipsy,
 And lived upon the moors:
Her bed it was the brown heath turf,
 And her house was out of doors.

Her apples were swart blackberries,
 Her currants pods o'broom;
Her wind was dew of the wild white rose,
 Her book a churchyard tomb.

Her Brothers were the craggy hills,
 Her Sisters larchen trees;
Alone with her great family
 She lived as she did please.

No breakfast had she many a morn,
 No dinner many a noon,
And 'stead of supper she would stare
 Full hard against the Moon.

But every morn of woodbine fresh
  She made her garlanding,
And every night the dark glen Yew
  She wove, and she would sing.

And with her fingers, old and brown,
  She plaited Mats o' Rushes,
And gave them to the Cottagers
  She met among the Bushes.

Old Meg was brave as Margaret Queen,
  And tall as Amazon;
An old red blanket cloak she wore;
  A chip hat had she on.
God rest her aged bones somewhere-
  She died full long agone!

JOHN KEATS

# NOVEMBER

# AIKEN DRUM

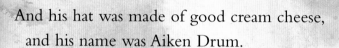

There was a man lived in the moon,
  and his name was Aiken Drum
*And he played upon a ladle,*
  *and his name was Aiken Drum.*

And his hat was made of good cream cheese,
  and his name was Aiken Drum.

And his coat was made of good roast beef,
  and his name was Aiken Drum.

And his buttons were made of penny loaves,
  and his name was Aiken Drum.

His waistcoat was made of crust of pies,
  and his name was Aiken Drum.

His breeches were made of haggis bags,
  and his name was Aiken Drum.
*And he played upon a ladle,*
  *and his name was Aiken Drum.*

There was a man in another town,
   and his name was Willy Wood;
*And he played upon a razor,*
   *and his name was Willy Wood.*

And he ate up all the good cream cheese,
   and his name was Willy Wood.

And he ate up all the good roast beef,
   and his name was Willy Wood.

And he ate up all the penny loaves,
   and his name was Willy Wood.

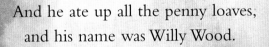

And he ate up all the good pie crust,
   and his name was Willy Wood.

But he choked upon the haggis bags,
   and there was an end of Willy Wood.
*And he played upon a razor,*
   *and his name was Willy Wood.*

ANONYMOUS
SCOTTISH

# HERE COMES A WIDOW

Here comes a widow from Barbary-land,
With all her children in her hand;
One can brew, and one can bake,
And one can make a wedding-cake.
    Pray take one,
    Pray take two,
Pray take one that pleases you.

# MISS MARY MACK

Miss Mary Mack, Mack, Mack,
All dressed in black, black, black,
With silver buttons, buttons, buttons,
All down her back, back, back.
She went upstairs to make her bed,
She made a mistake and bumped her head;
She went downstairs to wash the dishes,
She made a mistake and washed her wishes;
She went outside to hang her clothes,
She made a mistake and hung her nose.

311

 NOVEMBER

# GILLY SILLY JARTER

Gilly Silly Jarter,
  Who has lost a garter?
In a shower of rain,
  The miller found it,
  The miller ground it,
And the miller gave it to Silly again.

# MR. PUNCHINELLO

Oh! mother, I shall be married to Mr Punchinello.
To Mr Punch,
To Mr Chin,
To Mr Nell,
To Mr Lo,
Mr Punch, Mr Chin,
Mr Nell, Mr Lo,
To Mr Punchinello.

# GOLDILOCKS, GOLDILOCKS

Goldilocks, Goldilocks,
  Wilt thou be mine?
Thou shalt not wash dishes,
  Nor yet feed the swine;

But sit on a cushion,
  And sew a fine seam,
And feed upon strawberries,
  Sugar and cream.

 NOVEMBER

# LAVENDER'S BLUE

Lilies are white,
Rosemary's green;
When you are king,
I will be queen.

Roses are red,
Lavender's blue;
If you will have me,
I will have you.

315

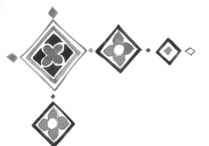

# THE FROG

A widow was baking in her kitchen and asked her daughter to go down to the well to fetch some water. Off the daughter went, down to the well by the meadow, but when she came to the well she found that it was dry. She wondered what she and her mother would do without water, for it was high summer and there had not been a cloud in the sky for days. And the poor girl was so anxious that she sat down beside the well and began to cry.

Suddenly, through her sobbing, the girl heard a plop, and a frog jumped out of the well.

"What are you crying for?" asked the frog.

The girl explained that there was no water and she did not know what to do.

"Well," said the frog, "if you will be my wife, you shall have all the water you need."

The girl thought that the creature was making fun of her, so she went along with the joke, and agreed to be the frog's wife. She lowered her bucket into the well once more, and sure enough, when she pulled it up, the bucket was full of water.

The girl took the water back to her mother, and thought no more about the frog until it was evening. Then, as the girl and her mother were about to go to bed, they heard a small voice and a scratching sound at the door of their cottage: "Open the door, my own true love. Remember the promise you made to me, when fetching your water down at the well."

"Ugh, it's a filthy frog," said the girl.

"Open the door to the poor creature," said her mother, for she was a gentle woman who liked to be kind to animals. And so they opened the door.

"Give me my supper, my own true love. Remember the promise you made to me, when fetching your water down at the well," the frog went on.

"Ugh, I don't want to feed the filthy beast," said the daughter.

"Give the poor creature something to eat," insisted her mother. So they laid out some food and the frog ate it all up thankfully.

"Put me to bed, my own true love. Remember the promise you made to me, when fetching your water down at the well," said the frog.

"Ugh, we can't have that slimy thing in our bed," protested the daughter.

"Put the poor creature to bed and let it rest," said the mother. So they turned down the sheets and the frog climbed into bed.

Then the frog spoke again: "Bring me an axe, my own true love. Remember the promise you made to me, when fetching your water down at the well."

The widow and her daughter looked at each other in deep puzzlement. "What would the creature want with an axe?" asked the girl. "It is far too heavy for a frog to lift."

"Fetch him an axe," said the mother. "We shall see soon

enough." So the daughter went out to the woodshed and returned with the axe.

"Now chop off my head, my own true love. Remember the promise you made to me, when fetching your water down at the well," croaked the frog to the daughter.

Trembling, the girl turned to the frog, who stretched out his neck obligingly. She raised the axe high, just as she did when chopping wood for the fire, and brought it down on to the frog's neck. When she had done the deed, the girl looked away for a moment, scared to see the dead creature and its severed head. But when she heard her mother's shout of surprise she looked back quickly. And there stood the finest, most handsome young prince that either of them had ever seen.

"It was me you promised to marry," smiled the prince.

And the poor widow's daughter and the handsome prince *did* marry, and they lived in happiness for rest of their lives.

### 📋 12 NOVEMBER

# THE WISE OLD OWL

There was an old owl who lived in an oak;
The more he heard, the less he spoke.
The less he spoke, the more he heard.
Why aren't we like that wise old bird!

### 📋 13 NOVEMBER

# THERE WAS AN OLD CROW

There was an old crow
Sat upon a clod:
There's an end of my song,
That's odd!

# FIRE ON THE MOUNTAIN

Rats in the garden-catch'em, Towser!
Cows in the cornfield-run boys, run!
Cat's in the cream pot-stop her now, sir!
Fire on the mountain-run boys, run!

 15 NOVEMBER

# BILLY BOOSTER

Billy Billy Booster,
Had a little rooster,
The rooster died
And Billy cried.
Poor Billy Booster.

 **16 NOVEMBER**

When fishes set umbrellas up
  If the rain-drops run,
Lizards will want their parasols
  To shade them from the sun.

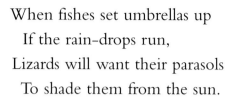 **17 NOVEMBER**

The peacock has a score of eyes,
  With which he cannot see;
The cod-fish has a silent sound,
  However that may be;

No dandelions tell the time,
  Although they turn to clocks;
Cat's-cradle does not hold the cat,
  Nor foxglove fit the fox.

 **18 NOVEMBER**

There is one that has a head without an eye,
And there's one that has an eye without a head:
You may find the answer if you try;
  And when all is said,
Half the answer hangs upon a thread.

##  NOVEMBER

O Lady Moon, your horns point toward the east;
        Shine, be increased:
O Lady Moon, your horns point toward the west;
        Wane, be at rest.

##  NOVEMBER

Hope is like a harebell trembling from its birth,
Love is like a rose the joy of all the earth;
Faith is like a lily lifted high and white,
Love is like a lovely rose the world's delight;
Harebells and sweet lilies show a thornless growth,
But the rose with all its thorns excels them both.

##  NOVEMBER

What are heavy? sea-sand and sorrow:
What are brief? to-day and to-morrow:
What are frail? Spring blossoms and youth:
What are deep? the ocean and truth.

# MY SHADOW

I have a little shadow that goes in and out with me,
And what can be the use of him is more than I can see.
He is very, very like me from the heels up to the head;
And I see him jump before me,
  when I jump into my bed.

The funniest thing about him is the way he likes to grow-
Not at all like proper children, which is always very slow;
For he sometimes shoots up taller like an india-rubber ball,
And he sometimes gets so little that
  there's none of him at all.

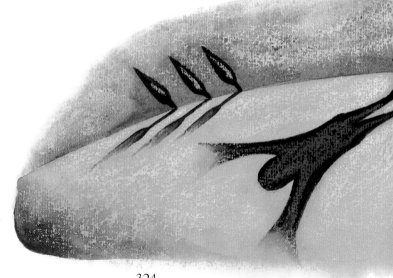

324

He hasn't got a notion of how children ought to play,
And can only make a fool of me in every sort of way.
He stays so close beside me, he's a coward you can see;
I'd think shame to stick to nursie
  as that shadow sticks to me!

One morning, very early, before the sun was up,
I rose and found the shining dew on every buttercup;
But my lazy little shadow, like an arrant sleepyhead,
Had stayed at home behind me and was
  fast asleep in bed.

ROBERT LOUIS STEVENSON

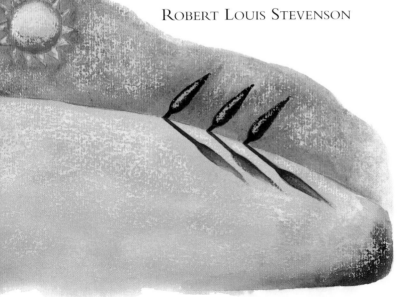

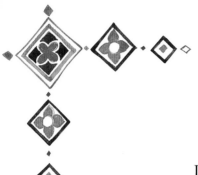

 NOVEMBER

# LIE A-BED

Lie a–bed,
Sleepy head,
Shut up eyes, bo–peep;
Till day–break
Never wake:–
Baby, sleep.

CHRISTINA ROSSETTI

 NOVEMBER

# HAPPY THOUGHT

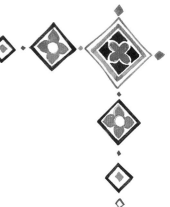

The world is so full of a number of things,
I'm sure we should all be as happy as kings.

ROBERT LOUIS STEVENSON

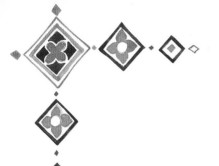

 NOVEMBER

# SKILLYWIDDEN

A man was cutting furze on Trendreen Hill one fine day, and he saw one of the little people stretched out, fast asleep, on the heath. The man took off the thick cuff that he wore at his work, crept up quietly, and popped the little man into the cuff before he could wake up. Then he carried his find home with care, and let the creature out on to the hearth stone.

When he awoke, the fairy looked quite at home and soon began to enjoy himself playing with the children. They called him Bob of the Heath, and Bob told the man that he would show him where to find crocks of gold hidden on the hillside.

Several days later, the neighbours joined together to bring away the harvest of furze, and all came to the man's house to celebrate the end of their task with a hearty meal. To hide Bob away from prying eyes, the man locked him in the barn with the children.

But the fairy and his playmates were cunning, and soon found a way out of the barn. Before long they were playing a game of dancing and hide-and-seek all around the great heap of furze in the yard.

As they played, they saw a tiny man and woman searching round the furze. "Oh my poor Skillywidden," said the tiny woman. "Where can you be? Will I ever set eyes on you again?"

"Go back indoors," said Bob to the children. "My mother and father have come looking for me. I must go back with them now." Then he cried, "Here I am mummy!" And before the children knew what had happened, their playmate Bob had vanished with his parents, and they were left in the yard.

When they told their father what had happened, the man was angry, and gave them a beating for escaping from the locked barn.

After this the furze-cutter sometimes went to Trendreen Hill to look for fairies and crocks of gold. But he was never able to find either.

# A GOOD PLAY

We built a ship upon the stairs
All made of the back-bedroom chairs,
And filled it full of sofa pillows
To go a-sailing on the billows.

We took a saw and several nails,
And water in the nursery pails;
And Tom said, "Let us also take
An apple and a slice of cake";
Which was enough for Tom and me
To go a-sailing on, till tea.

We sailed along for days and days,
And had the very best of plays;
But Tom fell out and hurt his knee,
So there was no one left but me.

ROBERT LOUIS STEVENSON

# THE LITTLE DOLL

I once had a sweet little doll, dears,
  The prettiest doll in the world;
Her cheeks were so red and so white, dears,
  And her hair was so charmingly curled.
But I lost my poor little doll, dears,
  As I played in the heath one day;
And I cried for her more than a week, dears;
  But I never could find where she lay.

I found my poor little doll, dears,
  As I played in the heath one day:
Folks say she is terribly changed, dears,
  For her paint is all washed away,
And her arm trodden off by the cows, dears
  And her hair not the least bit curled:
Yet for old sakes' sake she is still, dears,
  The prettiest doll in the world.

CHARLES KINGSLEY

331

# BROTHER AND SISTER

"Sister, sister go to bed!
Go and rest your weary head."
Thus the prudent brother said.

"Do you want a battered hide,
Or scratches to your face applied?"
Thus his sister calm replied.

"Sister, do not raise my wrath.
I'd make you into mutton broth
As easily as kill a moth!"

The sister raised her beaming eye
And looked on him indignantly
And sternly answered, "Only try!"

Off to the cook he quickly ran.
"Dear Cook, please lend a frying-pan
To me as quickly as you can."

"And wherefore should I lend it you?"
"The reason, Cook, is plain to view.
I wish to make an Irish stew."

"What meat is in that stew to go?"
"My sister'll be the contents!"
              "Oh!"
"You'll lend the pan to me, Cook?"
              "No!"

*Moral: Never stew your sister.*

LEWIS CARROLL

# GOING DOWN HILL ON A BICYCLE

With lifted feet, hands still,
I am poised, and down the hill
Dart, with heedful mind;
The air goes by in a wind.

Swifter and yet more swift,
Till the heart with a mighty lift
Makes the lungs laugh, the throat cry:–
"O bird, see; see, bird, I fly.

Is this, is this your joy?
O bird, then I, though a boy,
For a golden moment share
Your feathery life in air!"

Say, heart, is there aught like this
In a world that is full of bliss?
'Tis more than skating, bound
Steel-shod to the level ground.

Speed slackens now, I float
Awhile in my airy boat;
Till, when the wheels scarce crawl,
My feet to the treadles fall.

Alas, that the longest hill
Must end in a vale; but still,
Who climbs with toil, wheresoe'er,
Shall find wings waiting there.

HENRY CHARLES BEECHING

# A CHILD'S LAUGHTER

All the bells of heaven may ring,
All the birds of heaven may sing,
All the wells on earth may spring,
All the winds on earth may bring
  All sweet sounds together;
Sweeter far than all things heard,
Hand of harper, tone of bird,
Sound of woods at sundawn stirred,
Welling water's winsome word,
  Wind in warm wan weather.

One thing yet there is, that none
Hearing ere its chime be done
Knows not well the sweetest one
Heard of man beneath the sun,
  Hoped in heaven hereafter;
Soft and strong and loud and light,
Very sound of very light
Heard from morning's rosiest height,
When the soul of all delight
  Fills a child's clear laughter.

336

Golden bells of welcome rolled
Never forth such notes, nor told
Hours so blithe in tones so bold,
As the radiant mouth of gold
    Here that rings forth heaven.
If the golden-crested wren
Were a nightingale—why, then,
Something seen and heard of men
Might be half as sweet as when
    Laughs a child of seven.

ALGERNON CHARLES SWINBURNE

# I REMEMBER, I REMEMBER

I remember, I remember
The house where I was born,
The little window where the sun
Came peeping in at morn;
He never came a wink too soon
Nor brought too long a day;
But now, I often wish the night
Had borne my breath away.

I remember, I remember
The roses, red and white,
The violets, and the lily-cups–
Those flowers made of light!
The lilacs where the robin built,
And where my brother set
The laburnum on his birthday,–
The tree is living yet!

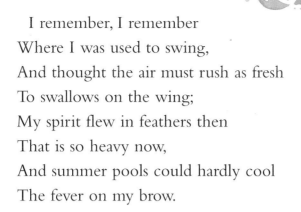

I remember, I remember
Where I was used to swing,
And thought the air must rush as fresh
To swallows on the wing;
My spirit flew in feathers then
That is so heavy now,
And summer pools could hardly cool
The fever on my brow.

I remember, I remember
The fir trees dark and high;
I used to think their slender tops
Were close against the sky:
It was a childish ignorance,
But now 'tis little joy
To know I'm farther off from Heaven
Than when I was a boy.

THOMAS HOOD

# MEET-ON-THE-ROAD

"Now, pray, where are you going?"
　said Meet-on-the Road.
"To school, sir, to school sir,"
　said Child-as-it-Stood.

"What have you in your basket, child?"
　said Meet-on-the-Road.
"My dinner, sir, my dinner, sir,"
　said Child-as-it-Stood.

"What have you for dinner, child?"
　said Meet-on-the-Road.
"Some pudding, sir, some pudding, sir,"
　said Child-as-it-Stood.

"Oh, then I pray, give me a share,"
　said Meet-on-the-Road.
"I've little enough for myself, sir,"
　said Child-as-it-Stood.

"What have you got that cloak on for?"
　said Meet-on-the-Road.
"To keep the wind and cold from me,"
　said Child-as-it-Stood.

"I wish the wind would blow through you,"
   said Meet-on-the Road.
"Oh, what a wish! What a wish!"
   said Child-as-it-Stood.

"Pray, what are those bells ringing for?"
   said Meet-on-the Road.
"To ring bad spirits home again,"
   said Child-as-it Stood.

"Oh, then I must be going, child!"
   said Meet-on-the-Road.
"So fare you well, so fare you well,"
   said Child-as-it-Stood.

ANONYMOUS
SCOTTISH

# MAKING A WIFE

In the village of New Abbey lived a man called Alexander Harg, and he was newly married. His wife was a fine-looking young woman, and some people thought that if the fairies got hold of her, they would kidnap her, so great was her beauty.

A little while after his marriage, Alexander was out on the shore fishing with his net. Nearby were two old boats, left stranded on the rocks. He did not go too near for he had heard stories of little people being heard around them.

Sure enough, before long, Alexander heard a noise coming from one of the boats as if people were using hammers and chisels in there. Then a ghostly voice spoke up from the other old boat: "What are you doing in there?"

"Making a wife for Alexander Harg," came the reply.

Alexander, astounded and terrified by what he had heard, thought of nothing but running back home to see if his wife was safe. He burst through the door, locked it behind him, and took his young wife in his arms. Then he went round closing all the windows and making sure that no one could get in.

At midnight there came a loud banging at the door. The wife got up to open it. "Do not open the door," whispered Alexander. "There are strange things afoot this night."

So they sat together quietly, and after a while the knocking stopped. But just as they were relaxing again, the animals began to make terrifying blood-curdling noises. The pair of them stayed indoors, and did not open the door until morning.

When they did so, they found a statue, carved in oak, in the shape and likeness of Alexander's wife. The good man made a bonfire and burned the effigy, and hoped never to hear the ghostly voices again.

343

# THE KANGAROO

Old Jumpety-Bumpety-Hop-and-Go-One
Was lying asleep on his side in the sun.
This old kangaroo, he was whisking the flies
(With his long glossy tail) from his ears and his eyes.
Jumpety-Bumpety-Hop-and-Go-One
Was lying asleep on his side in the sun,
Jumpety-Bumpety-Hop!

ANONYMOUS
AUSTRALIAN

344

DECEMBER

# THE EAGLE

He clasps the crag with crooked hands;
Close to the sun in lonely lands,
Ring'd with the azure world, he stands.

The wrinkled sea beneath him crawls;
He watches from his mountain walls,
And like a thunderbolt he falls.

ALFRED, LORD TENNYSON

345

# THE SNAKE

A narrow fellow in the grass
Occasionally rides;
You may have met him, —did you not?
His notice sudden is.

The grass divides as with a comb,
A spotted shaft is seen;
And then it closes at your feet
And opens further on.

He likes a boggy acre,
A floor too cool for corn.
Yet when a child, and barefoot,
I more than once, at morn,

Have passed, I thought, a whip-lash
Unbraiding in the sun,–
When, stooping to secure it,
It wrinkled, and was gone.

Several of nature's people
I know, and they know me;
I feel for them a transport
Of cordiality;

But never met this fellow,
Attended or alone,
Without a tighter breathing,
And zero at the bone.

EMILY DICKINSON

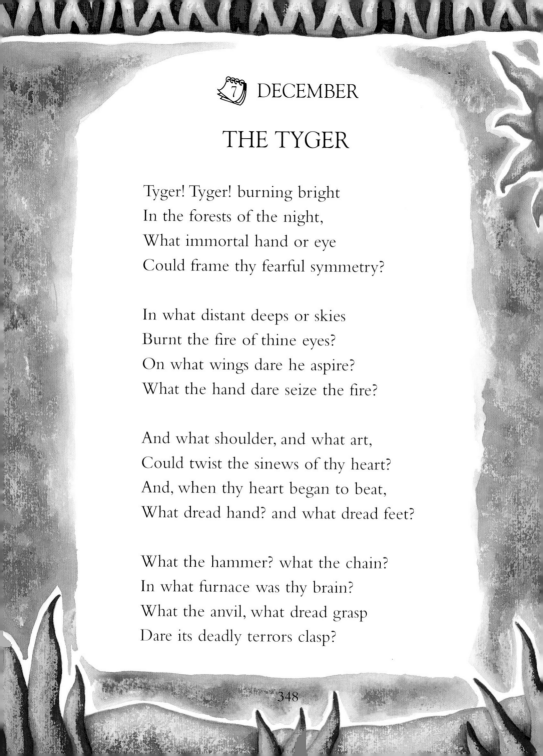

# THE TYGER

Tyger! Tyger! burning bright
In the forests of the night,
What immortal hand or eye
Could frame thy fearful symmetry?

In what distant deeps or skies
Burnt the fire of thine eyes?
On what wings dare he aspire?
What the hand dare seize the fire?

And what shoulder, and what art,
Could twist the sinews of thy heart?
And, when thy heart began to beat,
What dread hand? and what dread feet?

What the hammer? what the chain?
In what furnace was thy brain?
What the anvil, what dread grasp
Dare its deadly terrors clasp?

When the stars threw down their spears,
And water'd heaven with their tears,
Did he smile his work to see?
Did he who made the Lamb make thee?

Tyger! Tyger! burning bright
In the forests of the night,
What immortal hand or eye,
Dare frame thy fearful symmetry?

WILLIAM BLAKE

# THE CAMEL'S COMPLAINT

Canary-birds feed on sugar and seed,
  Parrots have crackers to crunch;
And as for the poodles, they tell me the noodles
  Have chicken and cream for their lunch.
    But there's never a question
    About *my* digestion—
      *Anything* does for me.

Cats, you're aware, can repose in a chair,
  Chickens can roost upon rails;
Puppies are able to sleep in a stable,
  And oysters can slumber in pails.
    But no one supposes
    A poor camel dozes—
      *Any place* does for me.

Lambs are enclosed where it's never exposed,
  Coops are constructed for hens;
Kittens are treated to houses well heated,
  And pigs are protected by pens.
    But a camel comes handy
    Wherever it's sandy—
      *Anywhere* does for me.

350

People would laugh if you rode a giraffe,
   Or mounted the back of an ox;
It's nobody's habit to ride on a rabbit,
   Or try to bestraddle a fox.
      But as for a camel, he's
      Ridden by families–
         *Any load* does for me.

A snake is as round as a hole in the ground,
   And weasels are wavy and sleek;
And no alligator could ever be straighter
   Than lizards that live in a creek.
      But a camel's all lumpy
      And bumpy and humpy–
         *Any shape* does for me.

CHARLES F. CARRYL

# MOTHER TABBYSKINS

Sitting at a window
In her cloak and hat
I saw Mother Tabbyskins,
   The *real* old cat!
      Very old, very old,
         Crumplety and lame;
      Teaching kittens how to scold–
         Is it not a shame?

Kittens in the garden
Looking in her face,
Learning how to spit and swear–
   Oh, what a disgrace!
      Very wrong, very wrong,
         Very wrong and bad;
      Such a subject for our song,
         Makes us all too sad.

Old Mother Tabbyskins,
   Sticking out her head,
Gave a howl, and then a yowl,
   Hobbled off to bed.

352

Very sick, very sick,
　Very savage, too;
Pray send for a doctor quick–
　Any one will do!

Doctor Mouse came creeping,
　Creeping to her bed;
Lanced her gums and felt her pulse,
　Whispered she was dead.
　　Very sly, very sly,
　　The *real* old cat
　Open kept her weather eye–
　　Mouse! beware of that!

Old Mother Tabbyskins,
　Saying "Serves him right",
Gobbled up the doctor, with
　Infinite delight.
　　Very fast, very fast,
　　Very pleasant, too–
　"What a pity it can't last!
　　Bring another, do!"

ELIZABETH ANNA HART

353

# TWO LITTLE KITTENS

Two little kittens
One stormy night,
Began to quarrel,
And then to fight.

One had a mouse
And the other had none;
And that was the way
The quarrel begun.

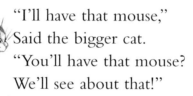

"I'll have that mouse,"
Said the bigger cat.
"You'll have that mouse?
We'll see about that!"

"I will have that mouse,"
Said the tortoise-shell;
And, spitting and scratching,
On her sister she fell.

I've told you before
'Twas a stormy night,
When these two kittens
Began to fight.

354

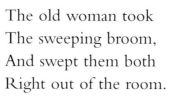

The old woman took
The sweeping broom,
And swept them both
Right out of the room.

The ground was covered
With frost and snow,
They had lost the mouse,
And had nowhere to go.

So they lay and shivered
Beside the door,
Till the old woman finished
Sweeping the floor.

And then they crept in
As quiet as mice,
All wet with snow
And as cold as ice.

They found it much better
That stormy night,
To lie by the fire,
Than to quarrel and fight.

JANE TAYLOR

# HARK THE ROBBERS

Hark at the robbers going through,
  Through, through, through; through,
    through, through;
Hark at the robbers going through,
    My fair lady.

What have the robbers done to you,
  You, you, you; you, you, you?
What have the robbers done to you,
    My fair lady?

Stole my gold watch and chain,
  Chain, chain, chain; chain, chain, chain;
Stole my gold watch and chain,
    My fair lady.

How many pounds will set us free,
  Free, free, free; free, free, free?
How many pounds will set us free,
    My fair lady?

A hundred pounds will set you free,
  Free, free, free; free, free, free;

356

A hundred pounds will set you free,
  My fair lady.

We have not a hundred pounds,
  Pounds, pounds, pounds; pounds, pounds, pounds;
We have not a hundred pounds,
  My fair lady.

Then to prison you must go,
  Go, go, go; go, go, go;
Then to prison you must go,
  My fair lady.

To prison we will not go,
  Go, go, go; go, go, go;
To prison we will not go,
  My fair lady.

# ALONE

From childhood's hour I have not been
As others were,–I have not seen
As others saw,–I could not bring
My passions from a common spring.
From the same source I have not taken
My sorrow; I could not awaken
My heart to joy at the same tone;
And all I loved, I loved alone.
*Then*-in my childhood-in the dawn
Of a most stormy life was drawn
From every depth of good and ill
The mystery which binds me still:
From the torrent, or the fountain,
From the red cliff of the mountain,
From the sun that round me rolled
In its autumn tint of gold,–
From the lightning in the sky
As it passed me flying by,–
From the thunder and the storm,
And the cloud that took the form
(When the rest of Heaven was blue)
Of a demon in my view.

EDGAR ALLAN POE

358

# ABOU BEN ADHEM

Abou Ben Adhem (may his tribe increase!)
Awoke one night from a deep dream of peace,
And saw, within the moonlight in his room,
Making it rich, and like a lily in bloom,
An angel writing in a book of gold:–
Exceeding peace had made Ben Adhem bold,
And to the presence in the room he said,
"What writest thou?"–The vision raided its head,
And with a look made of all sweet accord,
Answered, "The names of those who love the Lord."
"And is mine one?" said Abou. "Nay, not so,"
Replied the angel. Abou spoke more low,
But cheerily still; and said, "I pray thee then,
Write me as one that loves his fellow-men."

The angel wrote, and vanished. The next night
It came again with a great wakening light,
And showed the names whom love of God had blessed,
And lo! Ben Adhem's name led all the rest.

LEIGH HUNT

# THE BELLS OF LONDON

Gay go up and gay go down,
To ring the bells of London town.

Halfpence and farthings,
Say the bells of St. Martin's.

Oranges and lemons,
Say the bells of St. Clement's.

Pancakes and fritters,
Say the bells of St. Peter's.

Two sticks and an apple,
Say the bells of Whitechapel.

Kettles and pans,
Say the bells of St. Ann's.

You owe me ten shillings,
Say the bells of St. Helen's.

When will you pay me?
Say the bells of Old Bailey.

When I grow rich,
Say the bells of Shoreditch.

Pray when will that be?
Say the bells of Stepney.

I am sure I don't know,
Says the great bell of Bow.

# AGAINST QUARRELLING AND FIGHTING

Let dogs delight to bark and bite,
　　For God hath made them so:
Let bears and lions growl and fight,
　　For 'tis their nature, too.

But, children, you should never let
　　Such angry passions rise:
Your little hands were never made
　　To tear each other's eyes.

Let love through all your actions run,
　　And all your words be mild:
Live like the blessed Virgin's Son,
　　That sweet and lovely child.

His soul was gentle as a lamb;
  And as his nature grew,
He grew in favour both with man,
  And God his Father, too.

Now, Lord of all, he reigns above,
  And from his heavenly throne
He sees what children dwell in love,
  And marks them for his own.

ISAAC WATTS

## 16 DECEMBER

# SNOW

In the gloom of whiteness,
In the great silence of snow,
A child was sighing
And bitterly saying: "Oh,
They have killed a white bird up there on her nest,
The down is fluttering from her breast!"
And still it fell through that dusky brightness
On the child crying for the bird of the snow.

EDWARD THOMAS

# WINTER

When icicles hang by the wall,
  And Dick the shepherd blows his nail,
And Tom bears logs into the hall,
  And milk comes frozen home in pail;
When blood is nipp'd and ways be foul,
Then nightly sings the staring owl,
    To-whit! to-who!
    A merry note,
While greasy Joan doth keel the pot.

When all aloud the wind doth blow,
  And coughing drowns the parson's saw;
And birds sit brooding in the snow,
  And Marian's nose looks red and raw;
When roasted crabs hiss in the bowl,
Then nightly sings the staring owl,
    To-whit! to-who!
    A merry note,
While greasy Joan doth keel the pot.

WILLIAM SHAKESPEARE

# THE SUGAR-PLUM TREE

Have you ever heard of the Sugar-Plum Tree?
  'Tis a marvel of great renown!
It blooms on the shore of the Lollipop sea
  In the garden of Shut-Eye Town:
The fruit that it bears is so wondrously sweet
  (As those who have tasted it say)
That good little children have only to eat
  Of that fruit to be happy next day.

When you've got to the tree, you would have a hard time
  To capture the fruit which I sing;
The tree is so tall that no person could climb
  To the boughs where the sugar-plums swing.
But up in that tree sits a chocolate cat,
  And a gingerbread dog prowls below–
And this is the way you contrive to get at
  Those sugar-plums tempting you so:

You say but the word to that gingerbread dog
　And he barks with such terrible zest
That the chocolate cat is at once all agog,
　As her swelling proportions attest.
And the chocolate cat goes cavorting around
　From this leafy limb unto that,
And the sugar-plums tumble, of course, to the ground–
　Hurrah for that chocolate cat!

There are marshmallows, gumdrops, and peppermint canes,
　With striplings of scarlet or gold,
And you carry away of the treasure that rains
　As much as your apron can hold!
So come, little child, cuddle closer to me
　In your dainty white nightcap and gown,
And I'll rock you away to that Sugar-Plum Tree
　In the garden of Shut-Eye Town.

EUGENE FIELD

 DECEMBER

# LITTLE JACK HORNER

Little Jack Horner
Sat in a corner,
Eating his Christmas pie;
He put in his thumb,
And pulled out a plum,
And said: "What a good boy am I!"

 DECEMBER

# WHEN JACKY'S A VERY GOOD BOY

 When Jacky's a very good boy,
   He shall have cakes and a custard;
But when he does nothing but cry,
   He shall have nothing but mustard.

 DECEMBER

# LITTLE TOMMY TUCKER

Little Tommy Tucker
  Sings for his supper:
What shall we give him?
  Brown bread and butter.
How shall he cut it
  Without a knife?
How can he marry
  Without a wife?

# NOW THRICE WELCOME CHRISTMAS

Now thrice welcome, Christmas,
   Which brings us good cheer,
Minc'd pies and plum porridge,
   Good ale and strong beer;
With pig, goose, and capon,
   The best that can be,
So well doth the weather
   And our stomachs agree.

Observe how the chimneys
   Do smoke all about,
The cooks are providing
   For dinner, no doubt;
For those on whose tables
   No victuals appear,
O may they keep Lent
   All the rest of the year!

370

With holly and ivy
  So green and so gay,
We deck up our houses
  As fresh as the day,
With bays and rosemary,
  And laurel complete;
And every one now
  Is a king in conceit.

ANONYMOUS
ENGLISH

# THE LAMB

Little lamb, who made thee?
Dost thou know who made thee?
Gave thee life, and bid thee feed
By the stream and o'er the mead;
Gave thee clothing of delight,
Softest clothing, woolly, bright;
Gave thee such a tender voice,
Making all the vales rejoice?
Little lamb, who made thee?
Dost thou know who made thee?

Little lamb, I'll tell thee,
Little lamb, I'll tell thee:
He is callèd by thy name,
For he calls himself a lamb.
He is meek, and he is mild;
He became a little child.
I a child, and thou a lamb,
We are callèd by his name.
Little lamb, God bless thee!
Little lamb, God bless thee!

WILLIAM BLAKE

373

# THE OXEN

Christmas Eve, and twelve of the clock.
  "Now they are all on their knees,"
An elder said as we sat in a flock
  By the embers in hearthside ease.

We pictured the meek mild creatures where
  They dwelt in their strawy pen,
Nor did it occur to one of us there
  To doubt they were kneeling then.

So fair a fancy few would weave
  In these years! Yet, I feel,
If someone said on Christmas Eve,
  "Come; see the oxen kneel

In the lonely barton by yonder coomb
  Our childhood used to know,"
I should go with him in the gloom,
  Hoping it might be so.

THOMAS HARDY

# CHRISTMAS BELLS

I heard the bells on Christmas Day
Their old familiar carols play,
  And wild and sweet
  The words repeat
Of Peace on earth, Good-will to men!

And thought how, as the day had come,
The belfries of all Christendom
  Had rolled along
  The unbroken song
Of Peace on earth, Good-will to men!

Till ringing, singing on its way,
The world revolved from night to day,
  A voice, a chime,
  A chant sublime,
Of Peace on earth, Good-will to men!

Then from each black accursed mouth,
The cannon thundered in the South,
  And with the sound
  The carols drowned,
The Peace on earth, Good-will to men!

And in despair I bowed my head;
"There is no peace on earth," I said,
  "For hate is strong
  And mocks the song
Of Peace on earth, Good-will to men!"

Then peeled the bells more loud and deep:
"God is not dead, nor doth he sleep!
  The Wrong shall fail,
  The Right prevail,
With Peace on earth, Good-will to men!"

HENRY WADSWORTH LONGFELLOW

377

# A CHRISTMAS CAROL

In the bleak mid-winter
    Frosty wind made moan,
Earth stood hard as iron,
    Water like a stone;
Snow had fallen, snow on snow,
    Snow on snow,
In the bleak mid-winter
    Long ago.

Our God, heaven cannot hold Him,
    Nor earth sustain;
Heaven and earth shall flee away
    When He comes to reign:
In the bleak mid-winter
    A stable-place sufficed
The Lord God Almighty,
    Jesus Christ.

What can I give him,
  Poor as I am?
If I were a shepherd
  I would bring a lamb;
If I were a wise man
  I would do my part-
Yet what I can, I give Him,
  Give my heart.

CHRISTINA ROSSETTI

## MAGPIES

One for sorrow, two for joy,
Three for a girl, four for a boy,
Five for silver, six for gold,
Seven for a secret never to be told.

## 28 DECEMBER

# LITTLE ROBIN REDBREAST

Little Robin Redbreast
    Sat upon a rail:
Niddle-noddle went his head!
    Wiggle-waggle went his tail.

380

# THE NORTH WIND DOTH BLOW

The north wind doth blow,
And we shall have snow,
And what will poor Robin do then?
                              Poor thing!


He'll sit in a barn,
And to keep himself warm,
Will hide his head under his wing.
                              Poor thing!

# IN THE TREE-TOP

"Rock-a-by, baby, up in the tree-top!"
   Mother his blanket is spinning;
And a light little rustle that never will stop,
   Breezes and boughs are beginning.
Rock-a-by, baby, swinging so high!
     Rock-a-by!

"When the wind blows, then the cradle will rock."
   Hush! now it stirs in the bushes;
Now with a whisper, a flutter of talk,
   Baby and hammock it pushes.
Rock-a-by, baby! shut, pretty eye!
     Rock-a-by!

"Rock with the boughs, rock-a-by, baby dear!"
   Leaf-tongues are singing and saying;
Mother she listens, and sister is near,
   Under the tree softly playing.
Rock-a-by, baby! mother's close by!
     Rock-a-by!

Weave him a beautiful dream, little breeze!
　　Little leaves, nestle around him!
He will remember the song of the trees,
　　When age with silver has crowned him.
Rock-a-by, baby! wake by-and-by!
　　　　Rock-a-by!

LUCY LARCOM

# THE CAT OF CATS

I am the cat of cats. I am
  The everlasting cat!
Cunning, and old, and sleek as jam,
  The everlasting cat!
I hunt the vermin in the night–
  The everlasting cat!
For I see best without the light–
The everlasting cat!

WILLIAM BRIGHTY RANDS